SEASON
OF SMOKE

The Jack Palace Series

Yard Dog
Carve the Heart
Season of Smoke

A.G. PASQUELLA

THE JACK PALACE SERIES

SEASON OF SMOKE

DUNDURN
TORONTO

Publisher and acquiring editor: Scott Fraser | Editor: Catharine Chen
Cover designer: Laura Boyle
Cover image: shutterstock.com/Lukas Gojda

Library and Archives Canada Cataloguing in Publication

Title: Season of smoke / A.G. Pasquella.
Names: Pasquella, A. G., author.
Description: Series statement: The Jack Palace series
Identifiers: Canadiana (print) 20200208349 | Canadiana (ebook) 2020020839X | ISBN
    9781459742529 (softcover) | ISBN 9781459742536 (PDF) | ISBN 9781459742543 (EPUB)
Classification: LCC PS8631.A8255 S43 2020 | DDC C813/.6—dc23

We acknowledge the support of the Canada Council for the Arts and the Ontario Arts Council for our publishing program. We also acknowledge the financial support of the Government of Ontario, through the Ontario Book Publishing Tax Credit and Ontario Creates, and the Government of Canada.

Care has been taken to trace the ownership of copyright material used in this book. The author and the publisher welcome any information enabling them to rectify any references or credits in subsequent editions.

The publisher is not responsible for websites or their content unless they are owned by the publisher.

VISIT US AT

dundurn.com | @dundurnpress | dundurnpress | dundurnpress

Dundurn
3 Church Street, Suite 500
Toronto, Ontario, Canada
M5E 1M2

For Emma

PROLOGUE

I sat on the beach next to the corpse and watched the waves roll in. Suzanne was safe, that was the important thing. On the other side of the lake, the sun was coming up. Light shimmered on the surface of the water. I looked over at the corpse. "Goodbye," I said. I got to my feet and brushed sand from my pants. Hopefully whoever found the body wouldn't be too traumatized. Early morning joggers or maybe a dog walker, the dog's wet nose sniffing at the body on the beach. I turned my back on the corpse and began trudging through the snow-covered sand.

CHAPTER 1

I like to say I'm not a killer because it helps me sleep at night. I've killed people, sure, but I'm no killer. Does that even make sense? I only kill in self-defence, or so I tell myself. I wanted to put that part of my life far behind me. I wanted to sit out on my porch in the country and whittle sticks while the sun went down and crickets kicked up a racket in the grass. Sometimes, though, life has other plans.

I was living about half an hour outside of Orangeville, Ontario, in a sway-backed trailer that had once belonged to my good friend The Chief. The Chief had vanished ten years ago. I liked to think he was drinking daiquiris on the beach under an assumed name and maybe a brand-new moustache, but deep down I knew that wasn't the case. The Chief was dead and gone for more than a decade now. I'd inherited his trailer, his barn, and his land, complete with tripwires and buried mason jars filled with rolled-up cash. I had been working all fall to clear the tripwires. It was slow going, poking around in the woods, jabbing at piles of leaves with a walking stick, bending down to snip rusty barbed wire with a pair of industrial strength clippers. I didn't want anyone getting hurt.

The recruits were waiting for me in the barn. I walked past a few trees that hadn't yet shaken off their leaves and tossed one of The Chief's traps onto the garbage heap. My boots crunched on the gravel driveway as I headed for the barn.

The sign above the barn door said PALACE SECURITY in huge red letters. The sign gave me the warm fuzzies every time I saw it. Is it possible to change your life? Hell, yes. I, Jack Palace, was living proof.

Marcus, my first recruit, was standing just inside the barn. He and I had been working a job back in the city, but the pay wasn't great. We stood around in front of a jewellery store, and now and then when a shipment came in we stood at the back while guys climbed out of Town Cars with jewellery cases handcuffed to their wrists. No one had tried to rob us since we had started working there. Avi, the owner, was thrilled with our track record and kept making noise about a performance bonus, but so far that bonus was just a distant dream.

We needed more clients and we needed more recruits. I had put some feelers out, but all my connections were still back in the city, so I'd put an ad in the paper.

Half my day's pay went to fuelling up the truck to get to and from the city. It would be nice to get some local clients and not have to make that drive every day.

Marcus shot me a smile as I walked in. "It's a good-looking group, Jack."

I nodded. There were two men and a woman lined up near the heavy bag dangling from the ceiling. This was where The Chief had trained me so many years ago. Right there by that bag was where I finally got the drop on him, or so I'd thought. He twisted easily out of my grasp and then broke my arm. A white lightning bolt of pain shot through my body, and that was the end of training for that day.

I smiled at the recruits. I wasn't planning on breaking any arms. I could almost hear The Chief snorting. "You baby 'em, Jack, and you're going to end up with a bunch of babies. You think anyone is going to hire a bunch of babies?"

"Hello," I said to the recruits. "Thanks for coming. I'm not going to lie to you, this job can be very demanding. We are going to train and we are going to train hard. Some of you might not make it to the end and that's okay. Maybe some of you have worked security jobs before. We're going to do things a little differently around here. Make no mistake: after I'm done training you, you will have the skills to survive. What's the number one most important part of training?"

The woman raised her hand high. I gave her a nod. "Safety," she said.

I nodded again. "That's right. We're going to work hard, but we're going to look out for each other. No one's getting hurt on my watch. You got that?"

All the recruits mumbled.

"All right." I smiled. "Let's get started."

Marcus took the pan off the stove. I could smell cumin, chili powder, and sizzling hamburger meat. It was Taco Tuesday, one day early. "So what do you think?"

I sipped my club soda. The bubbles chased each other inside my nose. "There's some promise there. Rafael and Beatrice seem pretty solid. David is a nice kid, but ... he's not the sharpest knife in the drawer."

Marcus pulled a tray of hard taco shells out of the oven. "I agree. Nice but dumb. Any word on the car dealership?"

I had pitched our services to a car dealership in Markham. The manager I spoke to sounded optimistic, but that might've been his sales skills talking. Decades of slapping backs and blowing smoke. "Nothing yet."

Marcus scooped meat into the shells. "I'm just saying. We can hire more people but if we don't have jobs for them —"

"I hear you. We'll rustle up some business. Don't you worry."

We sat at the Formica table near the window and ate our tacos. The driveway alarm chimed. We turned to look at each other.

"You expecting anyone?"

I shook my head. "You?"

"Nope."

We both looked up to the little monitor that was hooked up to the driveway cam. A tiny car was trundling up the drive. Almost subconsciously, I reached down and patted the knife on my belt. I glanced over at Marcus. "You got any shit?"

Marcus looked hurt. He shook his head. "Come on, Jack. You know I'm clean. I don't fuck with that shit anymore."

I nodded. On the monitor, the car was coming closer. I stood up, walked over to the counter, and turned on the kettle. Then I went over to the front door to wait.

I didn't wait long. The car pulled up to the trailer. The driver cut the engine and climbed out. She was in plain clothes, but I knew who she was. Officer Mary Ellen McBride, Orangeville Police Department.

I gave her a nod. "Officer McBride."

She stood by her civilian car and shot me a smile. "I'm off duty, Jack. Call me Ms. McBride."

"Would you like a cup of coffee, Officer? Or tea? I just put the kettle on."

"Sure. Tea sounds lovely."

I held the door open and she squeezed past me. Inside the kitchen, she nodded to Marcus. "Heard you guys had some excitement today."

I poured water for the tea. "Nothing too crazy. Training some new recruits, is all." I dropped a tea bag into the cup and passed it over to Officer McBride. "Bringing jobs to the community and all that good stuff."

"Jobs are good." I watched Officer McBride glance around the trailer, taking it all in. Most of The Chief's stuff was long gone, bagged up and lugged to the dump. My own decorative sense leaned toward the minimal. There was a shelf of books, a couch, a little TV resting on a TV stand The Chief had made himself. "There's some folks concerned you're running a paramilitary organization up here."

I shook my head. "We're security guards. We protect malls, jewellery stores, that sort of thing. It's all on the up and up."

Officer McBride sipped her tea. "So you're not planning to go back to jail anytime soon."

"That was a misunderstanding."

"You were in jail for a year. The assault charges were only dropped when the complainant refused to testify."

"I told you, it was a misunderstanding. An argument got out of hand. I was young and stupid back then."

"And now you're older and wiser."

"That's right. You want a cookie?" I picked up a box of digestive biscuits and offered it to Officer McBride.

"Yeah, sure." She reached in and grabbed a cookie. "Well, I'm happy you're keeping your nose clean. We had a lot of complaints about the last person who lived here."

I kept my face blank. She munched her cookie and finished her tea. "I'll be around if you ever need me."

"Thanks, Officer. I appreciate it."

Marcus and I stood by the front door and watched her go. He turned toward me. "What was that about?"

"A nice quiet show of force." I squinted at the car as it disappeared down the driveway. "Officer McBride doesn't want us to forget the natural order of things. We're crooks and she's a cop."

"That's what she thinks."

"That's right. The way she keeps poking around out here, I'm sure she thinks Palace Security is cover for something else."

"Paramilitary organization."

I shook my head. "Nah, I'm pretty sure she knew that was bullshit. Some folks around here remember The Chief. They're still a little skittish." I grinned. "The Chief wasn't exactly a good neighbour." I remembered the parties, the music, the guns going off at three in the morning. "We're going to disappoint Officer McBride, though. We're going to stay nice and quiet."

After we did the dishes, Marcus and I sat out on the trailer's front porch. I sharpened my knife, dragging the blade against the whetstone. A flying V of Canada geese went by, heading south. Marcus tilted his chin. "That's smart," he said. "If I had the money, that's what I would do. Just pack up and head south every fall. Wouldn't come back until the snow melts."

I smiled. "Then you wouldn't get to talk to your neighbours about how much winter sucks."

"That's A-okay with me."

"Some people like the winter. The sun sparkling off the snow, the crisp smell of the air, the quiet of the woods …"

Marcus glanced over at me. "Sounds like you like winter, Jack."

"I don't mind the cold." I glanced up at the setting sun. "It's the dark that gets me."

Marcus nodded. "It's not too late to book tickets south. According to the *Farmer's Almanac*, we're in for a rough winter."

The sunset faded. I shivered. The darkness was closing in.

CHAPTER 2

The uniform was nothing to write home about, but hopefully it got the point across. Navy-blue pants and shirt, with *Palace Security* in black letters on an all-white oval just above the heart. I stood in the jewellery store and stared at the single customer. The customer looked up, made eye contact with me, and quickly looked away. I took two steps closer. The customer smiled at Avi behind the counter, thanked him, then hustled out the door.

Avi walked around the counter and looked up at me. He was short, about five foot nothing to my six foot four. His mouth was smiling, but his eyes weren't. "Jack, you got a minute?"

"Yeah, sure, Avi. What's up?"

"You know I like you, right? Since you've been here, we haven't had any trouble."

I nodded. Experience told me another shoe would be dropping right about now. "But Ike, he sees things differently." Avi shrugged. "Ike's hard-nosed. A pragmatist. He sees sales slipping, he thinks, what are we doing wrong? He looks at the numbers and he thinks he's figured it out. He says to me, Avi, it's the security man. He's scaring the customers. I say, no, that's Jack, he's a good guy. Ike says, I don't care how good he is. He could be Mother Teresa herself. People take one look at him and they run out of the store." Avi held up his hands. "You and I, we know this isn't true. You scare off the criminals, the thieves. The boosters with sticky fingers. But Ike, you know, he's always got his eye on the bottom line." Avi smiled. "That's why we work well together. I'm the dreamer, the big-picture guy. Ike's the number cruncher, the financial wizard. Together, we make it work."

I stared down at Avi. "And Ike's numbers are telling him I'm a liability."

Avi shrugged. "I tell him and tell him, you can't skimp on quality. We sell the best gold, the best stones. Our security should be the best, too. Ike, he doesn't see it that way." Avi reached out and patted my arm. "I'm sorry, Jack. You know if it was up to me …"

"We can lower our rates," I blurted. "Special November discount."

Avi nodded. "I appreciate you trying to meet us halfway here. Ike, though … his mind is made up."

I finished my shift. I felt numb. Customers came and customers went. An old lady argued with Avi over the price of a necklace. A happy couple bought engagement rings. Everyone's words sounded distant and underwater. Remember in the Charlie Brown cartoons, how all the adults sounded like sad trombones? That's how Avi and his customers sounded. By the end of my shift, I was actually hoping for some stickup boys to come in and jam some pistols under Avi's nose. Then I could jump into action, kick some ass, and prove my worth. No one came in. During the last hour, the store was dead.

Avi pulled out some Windex and spritzed the display counter. "Let's pack it in a little early today." He gestured toward the case. "We got some nice watches in the other day. You want one? With the employee discount, of course."

"Nah. Thanks, though." I said goodbye, shook Avi's hand, and walked outside into the cold and the grey. The sky was the color of slate. It seemed to hang just inches above my head, ready to drop down and crush me at any minute. I walked past skeletal trees, heading back to the parking lot where I had parked my truck. I had to drum up some more business, and fast.

I sat in the truck and I called the manager of the Markham car lot. "Bill! It's Jack. How are you? I was wondering if you'd had a chance to think about my proposal the other day. Uh-huh. Yeah. No, that's cool, I understand. I hope you'll keep Palace Security in mind for the future. Yeah. Thanks a lot."

I hung up the phone and sat there in my Palace Security uniform in my Palace Security truck. I could feel my dream circling the drain. It wasn't a good feeling. I wanted to drive back to the country and pile all the uniforms, business cards, and stationery onto the truck, douse the whole thing with gasoline, then light a match. While the whole thing burned, walk away without looking back. Once the flames reached the gas tank, that would be that. Goodbye, Palace Security.

Instead, I drove back to the country and parked the truck by the barn. I heard voices when I stepped out of the truck. I walked into the barn, and there were Marcus and Beatrice. Beatrice was working the heavy bag. Her feet were too close together.

"You need to work on your stance. Like this." I showed her. "Keep your head low. Don't punch with your hand, punch with your arm. Try to picture your fist going right through the bag. Go on, give it a try. Nice!"

Beatrice grinned. She walloped the bag.

Afterward, she stood outside the barn smoking a cigarette. She offered the pack to Marcus and myself, but we passed. I had quit smoking decades earlier. There had been some backsliding over the years, usually when drinking, occasionally just after sex. Smoking was a dirty, expensive habit, though, and I didn't miss it.

Drinking was another story. I had five months of sobriety under my belt, and I still dreamed of getting drunk every night. I'm talking about literal dreams where I found myself in some shadowy bar, sitting on a stool next to all the other rummies, a glass of something — usually Scotch — resting on the bar in front of me. Sometimes I was at a party, boozing it up and laughing with people from my past. Eddie, Grover, Suzanne. In my dreams there was always a moment when I realized I shouldn't be drinking, and that was when the guilt set in.

Beatrice pulled on her cigarette and smiled. "I know I should quit. I'm getting there."

I nodded. "It's hard."

"Yeah, it is. But I want to set a good example for my kids."

"How old are they?"

"Jamie's six and Travis is seventeen. He's autistic. Doesn't talk much. He loves to sing, though. He loves music in general. I've got him in a real good music therapy program. It's not cheap, though." Beatrice looked around for a spot to grind out her cigarette. I picked up a rusty old can and passed it over to her. She ground out the cigarette on the inside of the can and then dropped in the butt. "Travis's dad is long gone. Jamie's dad does what he can, but his hours are getting cut. We both work at the supermarket." Beatrice smiled. "I'm hoping, you know, to expand my skills. Make a little extra money. If I have to kick some ass while doing it, that's okay with me."

I grinned. "Security work's not like the movies. It's mostly a whole lot of standing around waiting for something to happen."

Beatrice lit up another cigarette. "I've been standing around waiting for something to happen my whole life."

Even with most of The Chief's shit hauled off to the dump, the trailer was still too small. In the summer months it had been fine, but now winter was closing in. Marcus and I sat bundled in our coats on the porch, sipping peppermint tea. "We lost our biggest client today."

Marcus looked over at me. I could almost hear his brain working, trying to figure out if I was joking. Finally he said, "Really?"

"Yeah." I sipped my tea. There was a bit too much sugar in it but it was warming me up. "Maybe we'll bounce back, maybe not. It might be time for you to think about other options."

Marcus was quiet for a minute. "You know, I've got family in Halifax. I've been thinking about moving out there."

I nodded. "Halifax is nice." I was there in August once, years ago. It was one of the most beautiful places I had ever been. Halifax in wintertime, though, is a different story. The wet, cold wind blows off the ocean and dumps snow all over everything. "It's probably safe for you to go back to Toronto, too. If you wanted to."

Marcus smiled. "I don't like the sound of that 'probably.'"

"That's life, though, isn't it? It's all one big 'probably.' No one really knows what's going to happen next." I glanced over at Marcus. "Maybe there's some people in Toronto still pissed at you, maybe not. All I know for sure is that if you're sitting here waiting for someone to roll out a red carpet for you, you're going to be sitting here for a long, long time."

Marcus was silent for a minute. He and my ex-girlfriend Melody had been involved in a cocaine-dealing scheme that had gone a bit sideways. Melody had ripped off four kilos of coke from her father, an old biker named Walter, and one of Walter's old road buddies, a psycho named Fisher. Fisher was gone, shot to death in his boss's old penthouse. Last I heard, Melody had gone north, cooling her heels in cottage country. Walter was still in the city, running his bar and smoking his hash.

Did he harbour a grudge against Marcus? Finding out his own daughter had ripped him off had almost killed the old biker. Would he take that pain out on Marcus? The fact that we had been up here in the country for four months without a visit from Walter and his buddies suggested to me that Marcus was safe. He was right, though — there were no certainties. Marcus going back to the city might be rolling the dice with his own life.

"Maybe we'll get some new clients."

I nodded. "I'm working on it."

"I want this to work."

"Yeah," I said. "Me, too."

Marcus looked off toward the grass. "I've been thinking of moving out. You've been awfully nice letting me crash here."

Truth was, I liked having Marcus around. Without him it would just be me in the trailer with the ghosts of the past. Me and The Chief's ghost playing cards, drinking whisky, watching TV. My days of having whisky for breakfast were behind me. "You know you're welcome to stay for as long as you want."

Marcus smiled. "Thanks, I appreciate it. But we both know this is just temporary."

The wind flattened the grass. Even with my big coat on, I was getting cold. I stood up, carrying my empty teacup. "Everything is."

CHAPTER 3

The next day, I drove back to the city. Winding country roads turned to multi-lane highways. Barns and fields gave way to strip malls and parking lots. A semi truck blasted by, missing me by inches. My pickup shook in the semi's wake. I could feel the traffic closing in.

I took the Gardiner Expressway east and got off at Spadina. I drove north toward Chinatown to see my buddy Eddie Yao. My old stomping grounds. I'd lived here for more than a decade, camped out in my office above a Chinese restaurant, which was above Eddie's illegal basement casino. He owned the restaurant and my office, too. He owned the whole building, including the stretch of rooftop where we had set up several old lawn chairs and a red and white Coleman cooler we kept stocked with beer. We called it the asphalt beach.

Eddie was in the restaurant. He looked up and smiled when he saw me coming. I pointed toward the roof. Eddie nodded. Together, we headed up.

Eddie popped the top off a beer, walked over to the roof's edge, and looked down. I joined him at the edge. Three stories down, the shopping crowds swirled past storefronts and vegetable stands. Everyone was wearing heavy grey and black and dark-blue coats. I wondered if maybe more colour would help the winter go down smooth.

"Hey, Eddie."

"Yeah?"

"Why not tropical-print parkas? Heavy puffy ski jackets complete with parrots and palm fronds. Why, in a dark season, do the clothes have to be dark, too?"

Eddie laughed. "You designing clothes now? Make a sketch of your tropical parka. I'll get my Aunt Camille to sew it up."

We turned away from the edge and went back to our lawn chairs. "You should come out to the country sometime. You can have some beers on the porch and watch the sun go down."

Eddie nodded. "Sounds pretty good to me. But, you know. The casino won't run itself."

I stared down into my soda bottle. "That's actually one of the reasons I'm here. How's your security situation?"

Eddie looked at me and then glanced away. He paused before speaking. "After the robbery attempt this summer, I brought in some more guys. Damn casino's a fortress now, Jack. But, you know. A subtle fortress. No one wants to gamble and have a good time if they're surrounded by wall-to-wall goons." Eddie glanced at me again. "But you know me. I'm always looking for a few good men."

I drank the rest of my soda and set the empty bottle down with the others. "I'm not looking for charity here."

"Of course not."

"I just figured, you know, you've got a casino, I've got a security company."

"I've got an illegal casino. You've got a legit security company." Eddie stared at me. "If you want a job, you've got it. You know that. But if you're asking me, that means something's gone wrong."

"Aah." I made a disgusted sound and waved my hand. "Growing pains. The boys at the jewellery store didn't like my attitude. Claimed I was scaring the customers."

"You know what you should do? Get Cousin Vin, a couple of other guys, and some ski masks and shotguns. Go into that store and rob 'em blind." Eddie chuckled. "Then go in the next day and ask for your old job back."

"It's direct. That's what I like about it."

"All I'm saying is, you wanted out of this world. You worked damn hard to get out." Eddie smiled. "You bought a truck and everything. Don't let some hard times knock you back down into the dark."

Eddie was right, as usual. Going back to being a leg breaker in his casino might solve my money troubles, but I'd be right back where I'd started. And what about Marcus? And Beatrice? I'd be letting them down. Hell, I'd be letting myself down.

Eddie jammed his hands into his jacket pockets. "Let's go back in. It's damn chilly out here."

Downstairs, the warm red glow of the casino felt like home. Eddie's new guys were easy to spot, even if they were trying to blend in. That hulking guy with the dark glasses and shaved head sitting at the blackjack table. That skinny guy with the scowl and the scar on his face nursing a drink at the bar. There was a new dealer at one of the poker tables, too. I thought I had seen him before in some other context. Jail? One of Eddie's parties?

We bellied up to the bar. Vivian the bartender sauntered over with a big grin on her face. "Well, well, Mr. Jack Palace. You still enjoying that country life?"

I smiled back. "The fresh air is nice but I miss your smile."

Vivian set a tumbler full of Scotch in front of Eddie and then looked at me. I smiled. "Club soda."

"You sure you don't want a beer?"

"I'm good."

I thanked Vivian as she put the drink down in front of me. I scanned the room. The tables were half-empty. The real action would start later, when the sun went down. A cluster of men were trying out their best blank looks at the poker table. A man in a dusty tuxedo was losing at blackjack. A grinning man in a cowboy hat walked by with an iguana on his shoulder. Business as usual.

"Say, Eddie. You hear anything from Cassandra?"

Eddie shook his head. "You know Cassandra. That woman's a rolling stone." He shrugged. "She stayed in your old office for just about three weeks. Then she cleared out. Left me a nice note, though." He grinned. "She even paid rent."

"Hey, I paid my rent."

"I'm just busting your balls. You did pay rent. You even paid on time once or twice." Eddie stretched. "Last I heard, Cassie was heading south. She was going to play some legit games, try to win a button for the World Series. You know no woman has ever won the World Series of Poker?"

"Sexism in action."

"It's something, all right. There's still not that many women playing at that level. There's Cassandra, Annie Duke, Maria Ho, maybe Annette Obrestad … time will tell with that one."

I sipped my club soda. The bubbles burned down my throat. From where I sat, I could smell Eddie's Scotch. I wanted to distract the man and gulp down his drink the second his back was turned. But I was still trying to colour inside the lines. Plus I would never rip off a buddy. "So my office is empty."

Eddie stared at me. "You want to see it, for old time's sake? It's a storage room now. It's full of boxes." He sipped his Scotch. "You don't want to come back here, Jack."

The Iguana Man strutted past again. I gave him the side-eye. "Any other attempted robberies?"

For years, Eddie had operated under the protection of his Aunt Cecilia. She had passed away this past summer of natural causes. Her heart had finally had enough and thrown in the towel. Almost immediately, an inexperienced crew had tried to take down the casino. Eddie had protected what was his. The only people hurt were the would-be robbers.

"Not a one." Eddie raised his eyebrow. "You look almost disappointed."

"No. Quiet is good."

Eddie spread out his hand against the bar. "There's quiet, though, and there's too quiet. That country life not agreeing with you, Jack?"

I frowned. "Don't put words in my mouth."

"You just seem … restless. Is that fair?"

"Restless? Hell, I'm worried. I got to make payroll. My people won't work for free." Marcus had worked for room and board when Palace Security was just getting up and running. Beatrice wasn't officially hired yet, but I was putting her under the umbrella of "my people." I wanted to help them both. I wanted to help Beatrice's kids.

"If you want a job here, Jack, you got it. Like I said." Eddie's eyes narrowed. "I don't think that'll help your people, though."

As much as I hated to admit it, Eddie was right. I couldn't go legit if I was working at an illegal casino.

We sat there for a minute and drank our drinks. Eddie raised an eyebrow again. "I know legit people, you know. It's not like I only hang out with roustabouts and highwaymen."

"Roustabouts?"

"I'm saying I know people. I know a lot of people." Eddie shrugged. "Maybe some of them need security folks. It couldn't hurt to ask."

I smiled. "Thanks, Eddie. I appreciate it." Eddie had done tons for me over the years. I had saved his daughter from a kidnapper years ago and won a friend for life.

Eddie snapped his fingers. "Blue Moon Davis. You know him? He's got a warehouse over on Dupont.

Antiques, fine furniture, stuff like that. Gold-plated light fixtures for millionaires' ceilings. He's always thinking he's about to be robbed. If you can handle the paranoia, I can make a call."

"You know what they say. 'Just because you're paranoid doesn't mean they're not after you.'"

Eddie smiled. "Exactly." He pulled his phone out from his suit jacket pocket. "I'll give him a call."

CHAPTER 4

Blue Moon Davis was indeed a paranoid old coot. I met him at his warehouse, but he wouldn't let me in. We stood on the loading dock, our jackets flapping in the breeze. Davis was chomping on the most foul-smelling cigar I had ever smelled. The man kept wringing his liver-spotted hands. "Deliveries. That's where they get you. Why wait to unload when they can just take the whole truck?"

I gestured to the loading dock. "So I'd be working out here, mostly."

"Yeah. Mostly. You stand guard while my guys unload the truck. Keep your eyes peeled. Anyone comes up that doesn't belong, you get 'em to keep on moving." Blue Moon Davis squinted at me, the skin around his eyes going all wrinkly. "How did you say you knew Eddie again?"

"We're old friends. Almost twenty years now."

The old man nodded, seemingly satisfied. "That's good. It's good to have old friends. You can make new friends and that's good, too. But that history you have — you can't buy that."

"That's for sure," I agreed. I wasn't quite sure what I was agreeing to, but I needed this job. I felt the old me recoil. Nineteen-year-old me wouldn't be standing here on this loading dock begging this old man for a job. But then again, nineteen-year-old me had made a lot of mistakes in life.

Blue Moon Davis puffed on his stogie. "You want the gig?"

"Yeah. I want it."

"Good. It's is yours."

I drove back to the country feeling pretty damn good. I had Jazz FM blaring on the radio, warm Oscar Peterson piano licks floating from the speakers. Palace Security would live to fight another day. A gig like this I could trust to Marcus or maybe Beatrice, even though her training wasn't complete. Was anyone's training ever complete? With any luck, we all keep learning until our bodies hit the dirt.

In the distance, a column of smoke hung in the air. It looked unreal, like a bad matte painting from an old-fashioned movie. The smoke wasn't moving at all.

I kept driving and the jazz kept playing. The column of smoke got bigger as I drove closer. It still looked fake. Just hanging there on the horizon. A fire truck zoomed past me, followed by another. I was heading directly toward the smoke. My stomach tightened. I was starting to get a bad feeling about this.

I pulled into my driveway and cut the engine. The fire trucks were already here. The trailer — my trailer, The Chief's trailer — was on fire.

My boots crunched in the gravel as I stepped out of the truck. I tucked my head down and strode toward the burning trailer. A soot-faced fireman stepped toward me and held up his hand. "Sir, you're going to have to stay back." In the old days I would've decked him. One punch, just enough to get him out of my way. But what was I going to do that the firemen weren't already doing? I didn't have a pumper truck, I didn't have hoses. I stood there in the gravel and I watched my trailer burn.

Where was Marcus? I asked the firemen but they said no one was inside the trailer. They hadn't found anyone, living or dead. One of them led me back to the fire truck. He had sandy-brown hair and kind eyes. He was saying something about insurance but I couldn't really hear him. Just like the people at the jewellery store, he sounded like a Charlie Brown adult. Nothing but sad trombone.

Eventually, the firemen left. There were ruts in the grass where they had turned the trucks around. I sat on the hood of my truck and stared at what had been the trailer. Now it was a blackened, soggy pile of junk. My clothes, my books — all that was gone, but that was just stuff. It could be replaced.

The smell of smoke hung in the air as I walked over to the barn. The door creaked as I opened it. Dust motes rose in a flurry, lit up by shafts of light. I cleared my throat. "Marcus?"

No one answered. I walked over to the ancient fridge and opened it up. The fridge light didn't go on. The inside of the fridge was cool but not cold. The barn's power was run from the trailer. That power cord was now a melted puddle of slag. I pulled out a beer and held it in my hand. *Five months, Jack. C'mon, man.* I put the beer back and exhaled.

I pushed the barn door closed behind me and walked around through the grass to the back. Marcus was there, crouching in the grass with his back to the barn. He squinted up at me, one eye closed against the brilliant sunlight. "Jack. I'm so sorry."

I crouched down next to him. "You're okay?"

"Yeah, I'm fine. But the trailer —"

I exhaled. "Fuck the trailer. It was getting a little tight in there anyway."

Marcus looked away. "I saw who did it."

My stomach tightened. "What?"

"It wasn't an accident. It was two guys in a red truck. A Chevy. I was in the barn. I heard them pull up. I was going to go see what they wanted and then one of them started shooting. Just plugging away at the trailer, *bam bam bam.* Another one had a Molotov cocktail. He lit the fuse, ran up to the trailer, and chucked it through the window." Marcus hid his face. "I ran, Jack. I climbed out the back of the barn and I ran like a fucking coward."

I reached out and grabbed his arm. "You're alive. That's what counts."

Marcus looked at me with his left eyebrow raised. Then he smiled. "I got the licence plate."

I nodded. "That might help." The truck was probably stolen, but I didn't have the heart to tell Marcus that. "These guys … did you get a good look at them?"

Marcus shook his head. "Not really. They looked like … just guys, you know? Two white guys in a truck."

"Did they …" I paused, trying to figure out the best way to phrase my next question. "Did they look out of place?"

"Like, were they city boys?"

"Yeah."

Marcus squinted, trying to conjure up a mental picture of the men. "Sorry, Jack. It's hard to say. They opened fire and I hauled ass out of there."

"You did the right thing." I stood up. The sun was starting to dip down toward the trees. A crow flew by, heading for its nest. "I got us a gig today."

"Yeah?"

"Pretty cushy stuff. Guarding a warehouse in the city. Antiques, stuff like that. It's yours if you want it."

Marcus nodded. "You can count on me, Jack."

"Let me borrow your phone."

Marcus reached into his pocket and handed it over. "You calling the cops?"

I shook my head. "Nah."

"They're going to want to talk to you."

I nodded. "I'm sure our friend Officer McBride will come looking for me. Right now, I'm calling a hotel. Unless you want to sleep in the ashes, seems like we need a couple of rooms for the night."

CHAPTER 5

The hotel was nothing to write home about. A row of eight rooms right next to Highway 10. A motel, not a hotel. The type of place you would stay if you were a meth dealer on the run with a dead body in the trunk. I stood outside on the concrete walkway next to the Coke machine and wished I had a cigarette. I didn't smoke, I wasn't a smoker anymore, but I still wished I had a cigarette. It was dark and it was cold. I bunched up my shoulders beneath my too-thin windbreaker. I didn't have to wait long. A sleek black Lexus pulled into the parking lot. The tinted window rolled down on the driver's side. Eddie grinned up at me. "Making friends everywhere you go, Jack."

I spread my arms wide. "You know me, I'm a people person."

"So what the fuck? Your place got torched?"

"That's about the size of it." I stepped forward and handed him a little slip of paper. Marcus had written down the licence plate number in a shaky childlike scrawl. "That's what they were driving. Run it by your guy at the station, will you?"

Eddie tucked the paper into his front suit pocket. "You know it was probably stolen."

"Yeah, I know. But was it stolen from the city, or were these local guys?"

Eddie's eyebrows shot up. "You think you've already managed to piss off the locals that badly?"

"Maybe it was a warning. 'We don't care for your kind, get the fuck out of here,' that type of thing."

Eddie frowned. "Yeah, maybe. Or maybe …"

"Maybe it was someone looking to cash in on the bounty on my head."

"You do have a way of making enemies, Jack."

"Sammy DiAngelo." I squinted. "He's got his nose bent out of shape over something that happened a decade ago."

"Maybe he's part elephant."

"What?"

"They say elephants never forget."

Sammy wasn't an elephant, but he was a dinosaur. He was a young guy but he had an old school conception of what a mobster should be. His motto was Never Forgive, Never Forget. His hatred of me had nothing to do with business. It was all personal, and it all came back to Tommy.

Tommy. He had saved my life more than a decade ago, when we were locked up together. A group of toughs came at me with mop handles, but Tommy called them off. He'd held sway on the Inside because his father ran rackets on the outside. When I got out, I owed Tommy my life. I'd tried to pay him back, but some things went sideways. Now Tommy was gone and I was still here. Mob guys like Sammy DiAngelo weren't too happy about that.

Cars passed us on the highway. A truck went by, hauling stuff from point A to point B. I watched it rumble on past. "We need to find out if this was Sammy or not."

Eddie patted his breast pocket. "I'll run this number and we'll see what's what. I'll talk to some folks, see what they've been hearing about Sammy. Don't worry, I'll keep things nice and quiet."

I nodded. "Thanks, Eddie."

Eddie peered at the dark night sky. "You should come back to the city, Jack. Not too many days left to kick back on the asphalt beach."

Beneath my windbreaker, my arms felt like ice. "Kick back with a hot chocolate, maybe."

"Do you ever miss it, the alcohol?"

"I miss it like crazy," I said. "Every damn day."

Eddie grinned. "I'm proud of you, Jack. Stay alive, all right? We'll find out what's going on."

He slipped the car into drive and pulled away. I watched the red tail lights of his Lexus fade down the highway, heading south toward the city. And then he was gone.

CHAPTER 6

I didn't sleep well that night. Every sound — a car rattling past on the highway, a raccoon overturning a garbage can — sent me wide awake, my hands scrabbling for the knife on my nightstand. I hoped Marcus was getting more shut-eye than me, but I doubted it. He had seen the gunmen live, in person. No doubt he was seeing them again every time he closed his eyes. Finally around three-thirty I went outside and knocked on his door.

"It's me."

The door slid open. Marcus peered at me from behind the chain. His eyes flickered to the left and right. Then he closed the door, unhooked the chain, and opened up again. "I can't sleep."

"Me, neither."

He pulled the door wide and I stepped inside.

There's a certain shade of orange I've seen only in motels. It's a sickly rust-coloured orange that reminds me of old faded photographs from the 1970s. Both the curtains and the bedspread in Marcus's room were that same faded 70s rust.

I sat down at the scarred wooden table near the window. Marcus sat on the bedspread. "I keep seeing the flames. I close my eyes and I can see them throw the Molotov. I can hear the whoosh." He shook his head slowly. "It's terrible, Jack."

"We can rebuild." I wasn't sure I wanted to, though. Clear the rubble, wheel in another trailer. One that didn't remind me of The Chief everywhere I looked. I spread out my hand on the empty table. "Last time I saw The Chief was in a motel room just like this. He didn't want to talk to me. He was busy drinking himself to death."

"And now his trailer's been burned to the ground."

I glanced over at Marcus. "It's just a trailer. It wasn't a museum. We didn't lose any priceless artifacts. Everything that burned can be replaced."

"Someone tried to kill you, Jack."

I leaned back. "Yeah, maybe. Maybe it was just a warning."

"A warning? A warning about what? Didn't those guys ever learn to use their words?"

"Seems to me like they were pretty effective communicators. Gunshots, Molotov cocktail — not a lot of room for nuance there."

"So what were they trying to say?"

"They were saying, 'Fuck you, Jack.'"

"Yeah, maybe." Marcus looked away. "What if they were after me?"

"Like, ripples from you stealing Walter's coke?"

Marcus shook his head. "I didn't steal it. That was Melody and you know it."

"Melody and I had some good times, but she's a whatsit. A narcissist. She only cares about how things will affect her. Plus, you know, she doesn't think things through."

"I'm just saying. What if Walter is still pissed? He's not going to send goons after his baby girl."

I shook my head. "This wasn't Walter. I'd put money on it. This is someone who wants me dead."

"What are you going to do?"

I stood up. I peeled back the rust-coloured curtains and stared out at the dark highway. "To start with, business as usual. You're going into the city tomorrow to guard Blue Moon Davis's loading dock. Think you can handle that?"

Marcus nodded. He looked pissed. "Of course I can handle it."

"Palace Security will need a base of operations. If this was summertime, we could operate out of the barn. But the snow is coming. That barn is going to be cold as balls."

"I've never understood that expression. Like, what the hell? Balls aren't cold."

"It's about cannonballs. Not testicles."

"Yeah?" Marcus smiled. "You learn something new every day."

I stepped toward the door. "Try to get some sleep. You've got a busy day tomorrow."

"Busy day wrangling antique chairs. One of those chairs tries to walk away, I'll be ready. Bust out my lasso and *boom*."

I stepped outside and pulled Marcus's motel room door closed. The cold air slapped me around a bit, but nothing I couldn't handle. I unlocked my door, walked inside, and closed it against the wind.

In the old days I would've sat right down at the wooden table and poured myself a drink. Two fingers of sweet brown whisky. No, make it four fingers. I suddenly flashed to The Chief's face, twisted up with rage and hate, shouting at me in a motel room just like this. That was the last time I'd seen him. Wherever he was now, I hoped he was happy.

I lay down on the bed and stared up at the water stain on the ceiling. It looked like a deformed rabbit. A mutant alien bunny, sent down to Earth to abduct weary travellers. I closed my eyes. Maybe if I pretended to sleep, I would sleep for real.

I must've slept because I woke up screaming. My hands were balled up into fists and my fingernails were digging white crescents into the flesh of my palms. Without thinking I grabbed the knife from the nightstand. I crouched on the floor next to the bed, breathing heavily with the knife in my hand. I blinked back sweat and tried to bring my breathing under control. Breathe in, count to three, breathe out.

No gunmen came piling through the door. No guys ran out of the bathroom swinging mop handles. I straightened up, still holding the knife, and walked cautiously over to the window. I lifted a corner of the curtain and peered out at the parking lot and the highway beyond. The sun was just coming up over the trees. A distant bird was singing. I took another deep breath and exhaled. *Good morning.*

CHAPTER 7

Marcus and I grabbed breakfast at a roadside Tim Hortons and then we drove into the city together. As we drove I regretted putting the big PALACE SECURITY sign on the side of my truck. I felt like I was driving a target and my head was the bull's eye. Marcus stared out the window at the trees flashing by. "When I was a kid, sometimes I'd go for long drives with my parents. I would sit in the back seat and hold out my hand like this, pretending I had a really long sword. Or, I don't know, a lightsaber or something. Everything we passed, trees, streetlights, houses, I would pretend to just chop 'em in half. Hi-yah! Just like that."

"Your parents still alive?"

Marcus nodded. "Yeah, they're still alive. They're out in Halifax. That's where my dad was born. His dad, my grandfather, was born in Jamaica. Dad's always talking about packing up and moving to Jamaica, but he never will. He's settled, man. He and Mom live near the harbour in a little bungalow just jammed with stuff. It would take a couple of sticks of dynamite to ever get them out of there. Maybe one day I'll move out there to be near them. They're not getting any younger." Marcus glanced over at me. "How about you?"

"I'm not getting any younger, either."

"No, I meant — how about your parents?"

"My mom is gone. I never knew my dad."

"You ever think about him?"

I was silent for a minute. The car tires hummed against the road. "I used to. When I was a kid, backed up against the wall of whatever shithole apartment we were staying in, I used to think sometimes that my dad, my real dad, was going to come busting in all handsome and backlit by the sun. Looking like, shit, I don't know, like a 1940s fighter pilot. Leather jacket, sunglasses, the whole bit. And he'd smile at me with perfect white teeth and say, 'Come on, son, I'm taking you out of here.' And we would go outside in the sunshine and there would be his motorcycle all shining and gleaming, and we would climb aboard and he would whisk me away to some glamorous, exciting life, like we would be international ninja spies or some shit like that." I shook my head slowly. "It never happened, though."

Marcus was quiet. "Families, man."

"Yeah."

I dropped Marcus off at the back of Blue Moon Davis's warehouse and wished him luck. Then I headed over to Eddie's.

The casino was buzzing when I first walked in. A balding man with mutton chop sideburns and smoky

1970s-style sunglasses had just scored big at the poker table. He grinned like the proverbial cat that ate the canary as his buddies hooted and slapped his back. I stepped over to the bar and nodded to Vivian. She poured me a club soda and pushed it across the bar. Eddie stumped up behind me and thumped my back. "What's the good word, Jack?"

"The Blue Moon Davis connection worked. Marcus is there now, guarding the loading dock."

Eddie eased down onto the bar stool next to me. "What did I tell you? Paranoid, right? Like he thinks a pirate ship on wheels is going to pull up to his warehouse and relieve him of his treasures at cutlass point."

I sipped my club soda. The bubbles tickled my tongue. "Don't say it like that. Sounds like I'm taking advantage of someone with a mental illness."

Eddie shook his head. "Not at all. You provide security. If Blue Moon feels secure, then you're doing your job right."

"Speaking of feeling secure, any word from your cop buddy about that licence plate?"

Eddie held out his hands, palms up. "Jack, c'mon. It's been, what, a day? You know how it goes. These things take time."

"You hear anything else?"

Eddie patted his pockets for his cigarettes and then pulled out a red lollipop and popped it into his mouth. He didn't smoke anymore, but the pocket pat was an ingrained habit that was hard to shake. "The usual bullshit." He heaved his bulk off the bar stool. "Come on, let's take a walk."

The wind blew cold across the asphalt beach. Eddie jammed his hands into the pockets of his suit pants. "I walk out here, instantly I want a cigarette. Isn't that something?"

"Patterns. Habits. I walk out here, I want a beer."

Eddie grunted. "Beer we've got."

"I'll pass. So you heard something?"

"There's been some rumblings about this guy Sammy. He's one of those My Dynasty Will Last a Thousand Years motherfuckers. He's trying to build an organization that will outlast us all."

The wind whipped my coat. "Sure. His guys can stuff his cash into envelopes and then leave those envelopes right on top of his grave."

"You know how these guys think. He's building for himself, sure, but also for his children and his children's children. You know, when the little whippersnappers are old enough to fill their father's wingtips." Eddie stared out at the city lights. "Sammy's cleaning house, Jack. Snipping off any loose ends. Your name is on that list."

"You think the guys in the pickup with the Molotov were from Sammy?" I shook my head. "I don't see it. Where's the finesse?"

"Something like this, you don't need finesse. You just need to get the job done." Eddie squirmed uncomfortably. "There's something else. I don't know quite how to say it."

"Just say it, then."

"They came to me."

I blinked. Eddie nodded. "Oh, they were subtle about it. It's not like they marched into the casino and slammed a briefcase full of cash down on the bar. It was two guys, average looking, no eye patches or peg legs or anything. They told me I had a nice place. I said thanks. Then they asked if I knew you. I could tell they knew the answer. They just wanted to see what I said. I said, "Who's asking?" They just smiled at that and said they were friends of yours. I could tell they weren't."

"When was this?"

"Yesterday evening. Right around dinnertime. I remember because Vivian and I were talking about getting some falafel from that new Egyptian joint. You should try it, Jack. Damn good food. They do this fried shrimp po'boy in this fluffy pita bread —"

"What else did they say?"

"They said they were friends of yours and they were looking for you."

"Did they leave a number, or —"

"No, nothing like that. They had a drink each, rum and Coke. Then they left." Eddie shook his head. "They didn't tip."

"Average looking, huh?"

"Yep. If you saw them on the street, you wouldn't think twice. Just two white guys, early thirties, unremarkable in almost every way."

I rubbed my eyes. Maybe these were the same guys who'd firebombed the trailer, but maybe not. Maybe there was a whole army of average-looking white dudes pounding the pavement, looking to take care of me permanently. In the old days, I'd have gone to talk to

Freddy. He was my man inside the mob. Freddy was gone, though. He was killed by my friend Grover. Grover had thought he was helping me, but he had fucked me good and proper.

"Who took over Freddy's spot?"

"You mean his joint on the Danforth?"

"Yeah."

Eddie narrowed his eyes. "Some guy named Bobby. You think he —"

"Let me stop you right there. I don't know anything for sure. I'm just asking. So you don't know Bobby?"

"Nah. I don't think he's anybody. Some low-level street solider they brought in from the cold."

I filed Bobby's name away. "All right. I'll talk to him later."

Eddie looked at me. "You know who you should talk to? Grover."

I shook my head. "I don't want to talk to him."

"C'mon, Jack. Grover knows these guys."

"Freddy was going to help me. Get me clear from this whole Tommy mess." I leaned toward Eddie and lowered my voice. "Then Grover slit his throat."

"Yeah. Well, Grover's not a subtle guy."

"No, he isn't."

"Still, he knows people. You know he wants to help you, Jack."

"Grover's help is going to get me killed," I muttered.

Eddie shrugged. "They're already after you. Grover couldn't make things worse."

I wasn't sure about that, but Eddie had a point. Sammy DiAngelo and his goons were coming for me regardless of anything Grover could say or do. "All right, all right. I'll talk to him."

"Good. I'll talk to my cop and see what's what with that licence plate."

"Thanks, Eddie."

The big man shivered. "Let's go back inside. I'm freezing my nuts off here."

CHAPTER 8

I didn't want to drive my Palace Security truck, so Eddie let me borrow one of his cars. I thought about scraping the sign off the truck, but then I thought, fuck it. Scraping off the sign would be too much of a concession. I wasn't about to bow down or give up.

I drove Eddie's pale-blue Honda over to Blue Moon Davis's warehouse. I pulled around to the back, and there was Blue Moon Davis himself hopping around the loading dock like an angry little troll. One of his workers was with him, a big guy who looked like he'd be more at home manning the velvet rope of some snooty club. The big guy loomed over Marcus. Marcus looked pissed off.

I hopped out of my truck. "What's going on?"

Blue Moon Davis turned to me, his teeth clamped around his stogie. His face was red. "What's going on? I'll tell you what's going on. This little —"

Marcus stepped forward, hands curling into fists.

"This little what? What? Go on, say it. Say it and see what happens."

I ran up the steps and got between Blue Moon Davis and Marcus. Blue Moon's warehouse worker narrowed his eyes and glared at me. I held up my hands. "Everybody calm down. Let's work this out. What the fuck is going on?"

Blue Moon Davis jutted his chin out at Marcus. "He's a thief. That's what's going on."

Marcus shook his head. "I didn't take shit and you know it."

I stared at Blue Moon Davis. Foul smoke rose from his stogie. "Marcus isn't a thief."

"The antique pen set on my desk. It's missing."

"When was I near your desk? I've been out here on the loading dock all morning."

"You went inside to the bathroom. You could've grabbed it then." Blue Moon Davis turned to me. "This is who you send me?"

"Marcus is a good man. There's been some misunderstanding."

"Yeah, I'll say. Tell him to give me back my pens and then the two of you can fuck right off."

I shook my head. "He didn't take your pens. The misunderstanding was on my part. When I gave Marcus this job, I didn't realize you were a fucking racist asshole."

The troll-like little man spluttered. His warehouse worker frowned and stepped closer. I glared at him. "We're leaving. It's up to you if we leave the hard way or the easy way."

The big man considered this and then stepped back. I thought Blue Moon Davis was going to have a stroke on the spot. "My pens!"

"They're around somewhere," I said. "Did you check up your ass?"

The big man swung at me. I ducked and then plowed my fist his stomach. With a groan, he doubled over. I waited to see if he would come up swinging, but my gut punch had knocked the fight right out of him. I stepped toward Blue Moon Davis and the little man cowered. "Don't hurt me!"

"We're leaving. We don't have your pens."

"Okay, okay!"

I gave Blue Moon Davis one final glare, then Marcus and I turned and walked down the concrete steps toward Eddie's car. We buckled in, I fired up the engine, and we got the fuck out of there.

The car engine thrummed. I looked over at Marcus. "You okay?"

Marcus stared straight ahead. "Nothing I can't handle."

"I'm really sorry, Marcus. I didn't know what he was like."

"Not your fault he's a racist asshole. When he finds those pens, you think he'll use 'em to write me out a nice apology note?"

We both laughed. I spun the wheel and sent the car gliding to the right. "Come on, let's grab some lunch."

We drove to a diner on College near Bathurst. My stomach rumbled. A pretty server handed us menus and glasses of ice water. She went off to deal with her other tables, then after a few minutes came back to us. "You guys ready?"

Marcus put down his menu. "Tuna melt on rye. Fries. I'm fine with the water."

The server turned to me. She had a beautiful smile. I handed her both menus. "Club sandwich on white, fries, and a Coke."

"Pepsi okay?"

"Yeah. It doesn't matter."

She smiled. "You'd be surprised. Once I had an entire table cancel their order and walk out. They had ordered all their food, apps and everything, and when I asked if Pepsi was okay, they said, "Cancel the order," and left. I couldn't believe it. They'd have to go to a whole other place and re-order and everything."

Marcus nodded. "Folks get serious about their sugar water."

The server smiled. "I mean, there's brand loyalty, but that's taking it to a whole other level. That's like some cult member shit right there." Her eyes went wide. "Oh, shit! Pardon my language."

All three of us laughed. The server sashayed away.

Marcus looked up at me and smiled. "Well, I guess we lost the Blue Moon Davis account."

I scowled. "Fuck him. We don't need his money."

"We kind of did, though, right?"

"There's a lot of racists out there. We don't need any of their fucking money."

Marcus leaned back. "So. Back to the drawing board."

"We'll find some new clients. And if we don't, well, at least we gave it a good try." *Peel the sign off the truck*, I thought. *Go back to work for Eddie. Go back to the underground.*

Marcus glanced toward the window. "I'm thinking about going back to school."

"You should. A little knowledge is a powerful thing."

He stared at me. "Did you ever think going legit would be so hard?"

"No, I didn't." I shrugged. "That's the game, though. There are hoops and we have to jump through them."

"I'm not just talking about pencil pushers and red tape, though. I'm talking about all of it. Racist clients, firebombers —"

I held up a hand. "Let me stop you right there. No matter what you do, they're going to be people who want to see you fail. That doesn't mean you have to roll over and play dead. It just means you need to try harder. You know why? Because fuck them, that's why."

Marcus grinned. "You ever thought about a career in motivational speaking? You know, if the security thing doesn't pan out."

"I could be one of those walk-across-hot-coals-on-the-beach type guys."

"I could see it. The Jack Palace Rules of Power. Stab your way to the life you want."

"Shit." I rubbed my close-shaven head. "If only it were that easy."

The server returned with our food. Marcus tucked into his tuna melt. "You could always retire," he said, with his mouth full of food. "One last big score and then sail off into the sunset."

"Move to an island and drink piña coladas until I'm firebombed out of my hammock." I stuck a knife into the ketchup bottle to get it flowing. "I've got to deal with some shit here at home first. And then there's you and Beatrice."

Marcus shook his head. "You don't owe us shit. You saved my ass, Jack. And Beatrice? You saw her. She's fierce, man. She'll get another job."

The ketchup gooped out all over my plate. I dragged two fries through the ketchupy goodness. Marcus reached for the ketchup and dumped some onto his plate, as well. The fries were delicious: crispy on the outside and creamy in the middle. I ate four more and then looked up at Marcus. "When I find the guys who bombed my trailer, things might get a little dicey."

Marcus smiled sadly. "Are you cutting me loose, Jack?"

"I'd say you're welcome to stay, but I don't have a place to stay anymore."

"That's okay." Marcus sipped his Pepsi. "I've got a place to stay here in the city. I'm gonna crash with some friends, listen to some music, smoke some weed, get caught up. They might have an extra couch for you, if you're interested."

I smiled. "I appreciate it. I think I've got a place, but if it falls through, I'll give you a call."

CHAPTER 9

Eddie grunted as he heaved his bulk up the stairs. How many times had I gone up and down these same dusty wooden steps? He looked over his shoulder at me. "I'm warning you right now, it's not like you left it, Jack. Cassandra made some changes when she was staying here, and then I basically filled the place up with boxes."

"As long as there's a place I can stretch out, I'll be happy."

Eddie reached into his pocket and pulled out a giant ring of keys. "Your couch is still in there. The new one, not the one you burned."

"I said I was sorry about that."

"Did you?" He unlocked the first lock, then the second lock, then the third. A security camera looked down at us from the top of the door. I tilted my chin toward it.

"That thing still hooked up to anything?"

"Nah. But we can see if we can hook it back up." Eddie pushed the door open and we stepped inside.

The smell was the same. Musty and dusty with a

new cardboard smell from all the boxes. My desk was still over by the window, but the plant I'd gotten when I got out of jail was gone. I had taken it with me to The Chief's trailer, and it had gone up in the blaze. I loved that plant. The desk looked so bare without it.

I rested my hand on a pile of boxes and looked over at Eddie. "Did I tell you they killed my plant?"

"Who? The firebombers?"

"Yeah. That plant didn't do anything to anybody." I glanced back at the empty spot on the desk. *I'm going to avenge you, buddy.*

Eddie shuffled over the window and cracked it open. A cold breeze floated street noise through the screen. Cars honking, people shouting, a woman's cackling laugh. He tilted his chin at the open window. "Don't keep that open too long or the pipes will freeze."

"It's not that cold. Not yet." I smiled at him. "Thanks, Eddie. I owe you one."

"Yeah, you do. But who's counting?" Eddie opened up the topmost box on a stack of boxes, reached in, and pulled out a fistful of bright-red lollipops. "You want one?"

"Those are the good raspberry ones? Sure, I'll take one." Eddie had a wholesaler friend he bought these lollipops from by the case. They'd helped him quit smoking and now he was addicted to sucking on sugar. Ah, well — a few canker sores beat lung cancer any day of the week. I stared at the room full of boxes. "Are all these filled with lollipops?"

Eddie shook his head. "Just this one, that one, and the one under it. Oh, and that one over there. You need anything else?"

"Actually, yeah. I managed to pull a few knives out of the ashes but I need more."

Eddie nodded. He unwrapped the lollipop and popped it into his mouth. "Then let's go shopping."

Eddie's Cousin Vin ran his hand over his shaven head. He had first shaved it for Eddie's Aunt Cecilia's funeral, then decided he liked the chrome-dome look. "Low maintenance," he told me. "Makes me faster in the pool. Sleek, man, sleek like a seal. What's not to like?" Vin turned to me and Eddie standing in the condo hallway. "This is your chance, Jack. Carl just got in some beautiful hardware from the States."

I shook my head. "No guns. But I do want to see his knives."

Vin nodded. "I knew you were going to say that." He turned and knocked on the condo door. The door swung open, revealing a man of medium height with round glasses and sandy-brown hair. Carl saw Vin and smiled. The two men hugged. Carl looked over Vin's shoulder at me. "You must be the famous Jack Palace."

I smiled. "Famous? Nah. You're thinking of Jack Palance. Crusty old cowboy actor, used to do one-handed push-ups."

Carl squinted. "Yeah, that rings a faint bell. Come in, come in."

Carl's condo was full of light. Even though the sky outside was grey, the condo was lit up against the darkness; tasteful lamps and ceiling fixtures bounced light around the white-painted walls. "Drink? Vin can tell you, I don't usually do business in my own place. Don't shit where you eat and all that. But for you guys, I can make an exception."

Eddie nodded. "Sure, I'll have a drink. Scotch."

"Just a water," I said.

I thought I saw a look of disappointment flicker over Carl's face. "You sure? I've got some really nice grappa. Friend of mine brought it back from Tuscany."

"I hate that shit. Tastes like spoiled grape juice and lawn clippings."

Eddie laughed and clapped me on the back. "Diplomatic as always, Jack."

"What can I say? People have different tastes. It's all good."

"Absolutely," Carl said. "All the more for me." He looked over at me and sized me up. "Vin tells me you're in the market for some knives."

"Yep. I know you're more of a firearms guy, but Vin tells me you've got some quality knives, too."

Carl reached under his coffee table and pulled out a silver metal case. He put it down on the glass coffee table and popped the latches. There were six knives in the case, nestled against black foam rubber. He grinned. "How's that for quality?"

I picked one up and felt the weight in my hand. I held it up and looked along the length of the blade. "Yeah," I said. "That'll work."

"You want that one?"

I tilted my chin toward the case. "I want them all."

Carl raised his eyebrows. He quoted a price and I counted out the money. Carl smiled. "These are friend prices, you understand."

I nodded. "I appreciate it."

"Any friend of Vin's is a friend of mine."

Outside, the sun was setting. Eddie and I walked back toward the Lexus. Vin stayed behind with Carl. I felt a little better walking around with the case of knives in my hand. It was strictly psychological. What is it the Boy Scouts say? Be Prepared.

We slid into the car and buckled up. Eddie turned toward me. "You're going to have to talk to Grover sooner or later."

"Where does he hang his hat these days?"

"He's been hanging out in your old bar."

I blinked. "Really?"

"Really and truly. He wants you to talk to him, Jack."

"Then why doesn't he pull his Batman routine and just materialize on my rooftop?" I still didn't know how he did that. Locked doors, armed guards — Grover could bypass them all like he was made of smoke.

"You know Grover. He's proud, Jack. Last time you guys saw each other, it didn't exactly go well."

"Last time I saw Grover, he slit my friend's throat." *Rest in peace, Freddy. You tried to help me and instead I got you killed.*

"He was —"

"I know, I know. He was trying to help me. He thought Freddy was going to hurt me. That doesn't change the facts. Freddy's dead."

"If it wasn't Grover, it would've been somebody else. Live by the sword, die by the sword. Freddy knew the dangers of this life."

"Maybe in the abstract. No one expects to die."

"And yet, we all do. Eventually." Eddie gunned the engine and sent the sleek car jetting toward Chinatown.

I hadn't been back to my old hangout in years. My ex Suzanne had been a bartender there. We met after I got out of jail. I'd watched her grab a baseball bat and deal with a rambunctious drunk and that was that, I fell in love. We had some laughs, then things went sideways and she ended up getting shot. It was only a flesh wound, but she'd gotten shot because of me. Just like Freddy, killed because of me. My life was too dangerous for the people around me. That was why I was trying to make a change. I tightened my fist. Thank god Marcus hadn't gotten hurt in the trailer fire. He could easily have been in there, eating an apple, watching TV — but he wasn't. Deep breaths. In, count to three, out, count to three.

"Drop me off at the bar."

Eddie snapped a mock salute. "Aye aye, your majesty."

"Shit. Sorry."

He shot me a sideways glance. "You want me to come with you?"

"Nah, that's okay. I'll meet you back at the casino. Hey, Eddie? Thanks again for everything."

CHAPTER 10

The bar hadn't changed a bit. As soon as I stepped through the door, I was hit with the smell of a million spilled beers. You weren't allowed to smoke inside anymore, but over the years every square inch of the bar had become saturated with smoke. The same tired rummies in their dusty plaid shirts were still hunched over the bar, muttering into their half pints. The lights were stuck on permanent twilight. Suzanne used to stand right over there behind the bar, her long dark hair pulled back in a ponytail, smiling as she flipped the taps and poured the beers. The bartender tonight was a man. I didn't recognize him.

"What'll it be?"

Beer. All the beer. A million beers. Just let me stick a straw down into the keg and drink. "Club soda."

"You got it." The bartender was in his late twenties. The sides of his head were shaved and he had a long sandy-brown goatee. Dragons and flowers and skulls twisted on his tattooed arms as he poured my drink and slid it across the bar.

I took a sip, feeling the bubbles fizz across my tongue. "I'm looking for a friend of mine. Little guy, little moustache, likes to wear white suits."

The bartender nodded. "Sure, he comes in here all the time." He craned his neck, scanning the crowd. I had already checked, but I supposed it never hurt to have an extra set of eyes. "I don't see him now, though. You want me to pass along a message?"

"No, that's okay. Either I'll find him or he'll find me."

I reached for my wallet but the bartender shook his head. "On me."

"Thanks, man."

I walked toward the door. It opened before I got there. I blinked. I was seeing things. Or I had a brain injury. Or the club soda had been dosed with LSD. Or —

"Hi, Jack."

I smiled. "Suzanne."

We found a quiet corner of the bar and hunkered down together, our foreheads almost touching. I could smell the dark vanilla smell of the bourbon she was drinking. I was working on my second club soda. "So," I said. "How's Saskatchewan?"

Suzanne smiled. "Really, Jack? We haven't seen each other in a decade and that's what you open with?"

"You know me. I'm suave and debonair."

"You're something, that's for sure." She sipped her drink. "Saskatchewan was nice. Saskatoon is beautiful. I went hiking a lot, right by the river."

"But …"

"No but. It was quiet and peaceful. I met a man, Steve. He had a forestry job. He was good for me, you know? Calm and stable. He had the patience of a saint."

Had, was, had — Suzanne's use of the past tense echoed in my ears. "You're not together anymore?"

She shook her head. "He died. Brain cancer."

"Shit. I'm sorry."

"The only good thing was that when the end came, it came quick. The docs told me there was very little pain." She looked up at me. She was smiling but her eyes were wet. "How about you? A few more scars, I see."

I touched my cheek. "I actually started my own security company."

"No shit?"

"I shit you not. Palace Security. It's a legit business. Got a sign on my truck and everything."

Suzanne reached out and put her hand on my arm. "Jack, that's great. No, really. That's really, really great."

"We, uh, we've had a few setbacks recently, but I'm trying to get it together."

"I'm sure you will." She sat back, staring at me with a smile on her face. "Jack Palace, businessman. I never thought I'd see the day."

"You know anyone looking for security work?"

She laughed. "I'll ask around. Do you have a business card?"

I patted my pockets. "Fresh out. So, are you just visiting, or …"

She kept staring at me. "I haven't decided yet." She tilted her chin toward my club soda. "You quit drinking?"

"So far."

She turned her head. A passing headlight shone through the bar's murk and caught her face just right. "I'm proud of you, Jack."

I ducked my head. "I'm trying."

She smiled. "And that's why I'm proud of you." She glanced toward the door and then back at me. "I saw Grover the other day. He was sitting right over there, with his back to the wall. It looked like he was waiting for someone. He kept glancing over at the door."

I nodded. "I actually came in here looking for him."

Suzanne didn't say anything, so I kept talking, trying to fill the silence. "Nothing major, you know. He just might have some information on some guys I'm looking for."

"Some guys?"

"Yeah." I bit the bullet and told her about my trailer getting firebombed. "We don't really know who or why. Could be a mob thing, could be local …" I trailed off. She was looking over my shoulder, her eyes slightly glazed. I had lost her. "Anyway, I'll get it squared away."

She nodded. "I'm sure you will." She finished her drink and stood up. "It was nice to see you, Jack."

I was all prepared to let her walk away, right out of my life for the second time. But fuck it, you only live once. "Can I call you sometime?"

She smiled. "Sometime, huh?"

"After I square things with the guys who burned down my trailer."

Suzanne stepped in and leaned in close. "Same old Jack. If you want to call me, then call me. You don't have to wait for every last little thing in the world to be right. Because let me tell you something, Jack. If you're going to wait for everything to be right, you're going to be waiting around forever."

She turned and strode away without looking back. I caught a whiff of her scent in her wake: warm vanilla cookies.

She was right, of course. I wanted to protect her from my risky life, but life itself was a risk. And love means leaving yourself open, leaving yourself vulnerable. Who was I really trying to protect?

The sounds of the bar bubbled around me. I sat there smelling the alcohol fumes wafting through the room. Maybe a Scotch. Just one. Not even a double. Just a single shot, no ice, glowing in the glass like liquid gold.

I got up and headed for the door. I reached for it, but for the second time tonight, it opened before I touched it. A little man in a white suit stood framed in the doorway. He looked up at me and grinned. "Jack."

I nodded. "Grover."

CHAPTER 11

"Mistakes were made. Let bygones be bygones. Water under the bridge, I say." Grover sipped his white wine and made a face. "This shit is terrible. Tastes like a melted tractor tire."

"This place isn't exactly known for its fine wines." We were sitting near the back of the bar, on the same side of a table, our backs against the wall. "So now you think Freddy was a mistake."

Grover pushed his wine away. "If I could go back in time, I would." The light from the bar glinted off his glasses. "I would've killed him a lot sooner than I did. It's like killing snakes. You want to wrestle with a king cobra? Or would you rather just squash that snake when it's still an egg?"

I stared at him. "You lost me."

"Freddy was no saint, is what I'm saying. If I could've gotten to him sooner, it would've been better for all of us."

"Freddy was my friend."

Grover leaned forward. "You want to see the best in people, and that's a good quality to have. But it can also fuck you up. Someone's shaking your hand, and in the meantime, they're holding a knife behind their back with their other hand. That's the way we live and you know it."

"That's the way you live. I'm done with all that."

Grover grinned. "No, you're not. I know you. You're looking for the people who burned down your trailer. Right? Oh sure, I know all about it. Word gets around."

"You know who did it?"

"If I knew, would I be sitting here jawing with you? No. I'd be out there with you, cracking skulls."

"What do you hear?"

"Same as you, no doubt. Sammy DiAngelo and his merry band of fuckwits."

I shook my head. "Whoever torched the trailer, they weren't pros."

"So who, then? You think it was just a couple of good ol' boys out burning down trailers for a lark? This isn't exactly swatting mailboxes with baseball bats. This is serious fucking business."

I frowned. "You don't have to tell me how serious it is. I could've been in that trailer. Marcus could've been in that trailer."

"If you ask me, it was local guys. And maybe they didn't even have a bone to pick with you. Maybe they were pissed off at The Chief."

"The Chief hasn't been in that trailer for more than a decade."

"Yeah, and maybe that's how they liked it."

I rubbed my eyes. "You're not making sense."

"I'm saying maybe it was someone who wanted that trailer empty. Someone who thought you were going to cramp their style." Grover pulled his wine back, drank it down, and made a face. "Look for local drug dealers. Bikers. Folks like that. Sammy and his crew would love to burn you out, but I don't think it was them."

"You know a guy named Bobby?"

"Bobby the Butcher? Bobby the Bear? Gold Tooth Bobby?"

"I don't know which Bobby. There's this guy named Bobby who's got part of Freddy's action. He's been running Freddy's joint out on the Danforth."

"Oh, Little Bobby."

"Is he actually little?"

"Naw. This Bobby's a beast. You want to talk to him? Say the word, I'll go along."

"I appreciate it. Don't think I don't. But that might not be the best idea."

Grover looked over at me. "This isn't easy for me to say. I'm sorry about Freddy. Okay? I'm sorry." He waited, but I didn't say anything. He nodded slowly. "You hear the forecast? Supposed to snow tomorrow. Batten down the hatches, Jack. It's going to be a cold one."

CHAPTER 12

The night was still young. I turned up the collar on my coat and caught the Spadina streetcar north to the subway. Then I headed east. After the Don Valley, Bloor turned into the Danforth. No one was really sure why Danforth Avenue was called The Danforth, but somewhere, sometime, the name had stuck.

My head was still reeling from seeing Suzanne. Had it really happened? Already the memory was dim and strange, like a dream. And then Grover right after. Had he been watching the bar? I didn't want to drag Suzanne into any of this. Grover, the firebombers — none of it. *Yeah, but what if she goes willingly?* Suzanne was a big girl, she could take care of herself.

Cold air whipped through my jacket as I stepped out of the Coxwell subway station. Flecks of snow were already in the air, haloed by the streetlights. I walked east, past a handful of diners and a Shoppers Drug Mart. Shoppers was lit up against the night. Everyone on the other side of the big glass windows looked warm and cozy. I tucked my head down and kept walking.

Bobby had taken over Freddy's coffee shop. In warmer times, there would be a group of old Italian guys outside, shooting the shit and sipping espresso. Inside, there would be a football match on TV — what Americans call soccer. This time of year, though, no one was outside. I glanced through the window as I walked past slowly. Two men inside, one guy sitting hunched at a table near the back, and another man — Bobby — behind the counter. The espresso drinkers were long gone, tucked away in their comfy beds. *Smart.*

The bells on the door jangled as I stepped inside. Luckily I wasn't counting on the element of surprise. Bobby looked at me and his whole face went sour, as if I were wearing a suit made of garbage. The man at the back table looked up. I didn't recognize him. Was he a civilian? Just an ordinary guy looking for a sip of grappa to warm his bones? Or was he part of Bobby's crew? I had to assume the guy was connected until I knew otherwise.

"You know who I am?"

Bobby stared at me. "Should I?"

"Jack. Jack Palace."

"Yeah." Bobby made a show of picking up a glass and giving it a polish. "I know who you are."

I nodded to him. "I heard you moved in. Looks like you haven't changed the place much."

Bobby just stared at me with that sour garbage look on his face. Then he nodded slowly. "Why mess with success?"

I shot the man at the back a look — *stay where you are, dude* — and then I pulled up a bar stool. "Give me a soda."

Bobby frowned. "This isn't the movies, man. You have to say what kind."

"What?"

"In the movies, some guy walks up to the bar just like you did and says, gimme a beer. Then the bartender pours him one. Like what kind of crappy bar has only one kind of beer?" He paused. "It's the same with soda. You gotta say what kind you want."

I stared at him. "Surprise me."

He grumbled but reached down and pulled a yellow bottle out of the bar fridge. "There. You surprised?"

I sipped it slowly. Pineapple. "I'll tell you what was surprising. Driving home the other day and my trailer was on fire."

Bobby smirked. I resisted the urge to smash the bottle against the counter and wipe that smirk off his face with the broken glass. "Yeah. I heard about that."

"You heard about that, huh?"

"Yeah. I just said I did."

I took another long, slow sip. "Word gets around, I guess."

"Come on, Jack." Bobby held out his hands, palms up. "What do you want from me?"

"There's still a price on my head. Did you know that?"

"Shee-it." He reached down and grabbed himself a beer. "Everyone's got a price on their head. Cost of doing business."

I heard a dry, rasping chuckle and glanced over. The man at the back table met my eyes and then, with a smile on his face, quickly looked away.

"So I'm just wondering, considering how good you are at hearing things, if you'd heard anything about the guys who torched my trailer."

"Even if I had, why would I tell you?"

"For old time's sake. Do it for Freddy."

Instantly I knew I had made a mistake. Bobby's already dark face clouded over. "Freddy's dead."

"I know. I'm sorry."

Bobby shrugged. "He knew the risks." He narrowed his eyes and stared at me. "You know who killed him?"

"No, who?"

"That's not a rhetorical question. I'm actually asking."

"If I hear anything, I'll let you know." I upended the soda bottle and guzzled the rest. I was lying. I knew damn well Grover was the one who had slit Freddy's throat because I'd been standing right in front of him when it happened. I hadn't wanted it to happen, but that didn't matter. Freddy was dead and there was no turning back.

Bobby scowled. His buddy at the back stood up and sauntered toward us. His hands were in his jacket pockets. *Always watch the hands*, The Chief had told me a long time ago. *They can't pull anything on you if you always watch the hands.* "Hey, Bobby," the man said, "can I get a refill?"

The man suddenly lunged at me. His right hand came out of his jacket holding a knife. It glittered as he slashed out in a long arc. I twisted to the side as the blade sliced through my sleeve. I blocked the man's next thrust with my elbow. He wanted to see me dead, bleeding out on the floor. *Not today.* I pulled out my own knife from beneath my coat and stepped forward. The man grunted as my blade slipped into his gut. I twisted the knife, pulled it free, and hit the man in the face with the hilt. The man stumbled backward, left hand pressed against his gut, blood seeping through his fingers, his eye swelling closed. He was still holding the knife.

Bobby was fumbling beneath the bar and he came up with a little pistol. I tried to keep the knife man in my sight while I lashed out with my knife, slashing Bobby's gun arm. The gun went off — loud, so damn loud — and the bullet thudded harmlessly into the ceiling. The knife man rushed forward, and I kicked him with my steel-toed boot. This time the man dropped the knife as he went flying backwards. Bobby was trying to transfer the gun into his other hand. I hit him in the face with the hilt of the knife, once, twice, three times, as hard as I could. He stumbled backward, smashed his back against the bar, then crumpled to the ground. The gun skittered across the floor like a cockroach.

I stood there breathing heavily. I could still smell the gunpowder. I glanced down at the knife man. He was conscious but groggy. I kicked him in the face and he went down and out. I crouched down and scooped up the gun. I was always surprised by how heavy the damn things were.

I shifted my knife to my left hand. The handle was sticky with Bobby's blood. I stuck my right index finger into the rip in my sleeve. The knife man had sliced the fabric but not my skin. If I had been one second slower, though, it would've been a different story.

I tucked the bloody knife back into my coat and turned and walked out the door. I was still breathing heavily, and the night air burned my lungs. The cold air was a shock, like jumping into a freezing pool. It was time to put some serious distance between myself and the two men bleeding on what had once been Freddy's floor. *Shit*, I thought, as I headed back toward Coxwell station. *Shit, shit, shit.*

CHAPTER 13

Eddie saw the look on my face as I strode across the casino floor. He hefted his bulk off his bar stool and met me by the roulette wheel. "You okay?"

I lifted my arm to show him my cut sleeve. "Those bastards killed my jacket."

Eddie didn't smile. His mouth was a thin, grim line. "Let's step into my office."

We stepped into Eddie's office and the big man shut the door. A lamp cast a warm yellow glow. There was the usual blizzard of paperwork covering his desk. He sat down, rummaged through a drawer, and came up with a lollipop. "You want one?"

I shook my head. "No thanks." What I wanted was Scotch. I wanted to ride a St. Bernard rescue dog down a mountainside, guzzling freely from the cask of whisky around the dog's neck. "You got any beer?"

"You know I do." Eddie opened up a little bar fridge and pulled out a bottle. He held it away from me. "You know beer has alcohol in it, right?"

I just looked at him. Eddie nodded. "I'm just saying, it's great that you're off the booze. I commend you for it. I know that shit's not easy. But don't fool yourself into thinking that beer is somehow better than hard liquor."

"Put it away," I said. Eddie smiled and put the bottle back in the fridge. "See that?" I said. "Total control."

Eddie squinted. "Sometimes I can't tell if you're joking or not."

"I'm mysterious like that." I picked up a lollipop and unwrapped it. "I'm like the sphinx."

"The sphinx?"

"You know. Giant statue, cat body, human head, stretched out all mysterious in the desert."

"I know what the sphinx is. I just don't think it's all that mysterious."

I let it drop. I crunched my lollipop while I gave Eddie the rundown of my encounter with Bobby and the knife man. When I was done, Eddie shook his head. "Whatever the price on your head was before, I have a feeling it just went up."

I grinned. "You looking to cash in?"

Eddie barked out a short, quick laugh. "You're not getting out of your bar tab that easily."

I stood up. "I'm going upstairs to crash. You know what they say, tomorrow is another day."

I sat on the couch among the boxes in my old apartment. The desk looked so bare without a plant. *Note to self*, I thought. *Buy a plant first thing tomorrow.*

I was no closer to finding out who had firebombed my trailer. Instead I had made a few new enemies, but I was used to that. Right about now Bobby was probably on the phone squawking to Sammy DiAngelo about how I had done him wrong. Sammy already blamed me for Tommy. The man wanted me dead. I'd have to settle the score with him sooner or later.

I kicked off my boots and stretched out on the couch. The neon lights of Chinatown shone through the window. I heard the hush of car tires going through the freshly fallen snow. And then I fell asleep.

When I woke up, I thought I was still dreaming. Grover was sitting in the dark near my old desk, wearing his all-white suit. The man glowed in the moonlight. "You know, Jack," he said, "I've been thinking."

I rubbed my eyes. "What about?" The door to my old office was solid steel with a thin wood veneer over it. There were four locks. The windows — one by the desk, one in the bathroom — locked from the inside. I knew better than to ask Grover how he'd gotten in.

His teeth gleamed white. "I say we settle this shit with Sammy once and for all."

I sat up. "I've never even met the man."

"I have. Once. I was on a job for Tommy's dad. There was a load of opioids being trucked in from the States, and The Old Man wanted me to boost it. No problem, I told him. A job like this, you only need a handful of guys and a dark country road. I got my crew together — you know JoJo? He's one of the best. He could steal your shadow right off a brick wall. I got my crew together and we set up by the side of the road. The truck came by and we boxed it in. The driver swerved, and I thought he was going to flip the truck, but he didn't. The truck went off the road into the dirt. The driver folded so fast I thought maybe he was in on it, like he had been warned we were coming or something. I don't know for sure. He was real passive when we tied him up." Grover grinned. "I wish every job was so easy."

"Where does Sammy come into it?"

"I'm getting there. Hold your horses. So JoJo takes off with the truck, and Pete and I follow in the cars we boosted specifically for the gig. We slide into one of The Old Man's warehouses, as smooth as butter. We climb out of the vehicles, and there's a freakin' mobster reunion going on. The Old Man's not there, of course — you know he always had insulation from all that street level shit — but his guy Left Foot Tony is there with some of his soldiers, including Sammy. Back then Sammy was a real loudmouth, hair slicked back, gold chains, track suit, real central casting shit. So JoJo slaps the keys to the truck into Left Foot Tony's hand, and then we're just standing around, you know, waiting for the payout The Old Man had promised us. And Sammy comes swaggering up all empty-handed and says, 'What if we don't pay?'"

Grover paused, looking at me in the dark. "Can you believe that shit? 'What if we don't pay?' As if now's the time to fucking negotiate. Well, JoJo gets all stiff-backed, and Pete's got his hackles up, too, but they both look over at me like they want me to step up and end this guy forever. Instead I ignored him. I turned to Tony and said, 'What the fuck is this shit?' I don't know if you know Left Foot Tony, but he's a real stand-up guy. He cooled Sammy out with just a look and waved one of the soldiers forward. Bruce, I think the guy's name was. How's that for a name? That's what they called the mechanical shark in *Jaws*, did you know that? Anyway, Bruce steps forward with a briefcase and it's all there, every single dollar we had coming to us. I couldn't resist sneaking a peek at Sammy as I walked off with the case. His face was red, Jack. I'm not talking about a brisk walk on a summer's day kind of red, I'm talking tomato red. The man was steaming. As if us getting paid for a job well done was some kind of personal insult to the man." Grover grinned. "Well, fuck him, right? We left and banked the cash, and that was that. I made sure to ask about him, though. Found out his name, his connections, where he lays his head, all that shit. Filed it all away in case I ever needed it. You know that old saying, keep your friends close but your enemies closer."

Grover sat back. The Chinatown neon streamed through the window. "Apparently he's changed his look a bit since then. Replaced the Adidas with Armani, that sort of thing. Now he's got a haircut that doesn't make him look like a fucking Oompa-Loompa. But by all accounts, he's still an asshole."

I leaned over and turned on the floor lamp. "So you say we should settle this. How do you propose we do that?"

Grover didn't blink. "Like I said, he's an asshole. If he goes missing, no one's going to cry too hard."

I shook my head. "I don't do that anymore."

"Right, I forgot, you joined the fucking Boy Scouts. You can't merit badge your way out of this one, Jackie

Boy. There's only one thing a guy like Sammy understands, and that's this." Grover held up a clenched fist.

"There is another way. We go to his bosses. Is Left Foot Tony still around?"

"I don't know, Jack. There was a shake-up when The Old Man shuffled off this mortal coil. Some of the old timers took early retirement, if you know what I mean. A bunch of low-level meatheads like Sammy DiAngelo got put into shoes they're not big enough to fill." Grover slowly shook his head. "A man's word used to mean something."

"Did it, though?"

He frowned. "What do you mean?"

I sat back on the couch and spread my arms wide. "It just seems to me that there was a lot of backstabbing and throat-slitting even back in the good old days."

Grover sat still for a moment. Then a smile slowly spread across his face. "You're not wrong." He stood up and dusted off the left arm of his white suit. "Sammy DiAngelo, Jack. Think about it. Soon all your problems could be over."

I didn't think whacking a mob boss was the best way to start over with a clean slate, but I kept my mouth shut. I waited to see if Grover would go out the window or just disappear in a puff of smoke. Instead the little man walked right out the door.

The red digital numbers on my clock radio said 4:43 a.m. Fuck it. I turned off the light and tried to go back to sleep.

CHAPTER 14

Sleep didn't come easy. I tossed and turned on the couch for about fifteen minutes and then I got up. I showered, shaved, and put on a clean suit. I didn't have a flower for my lapel, but I was feeling pretty fresh. Time to start a brand-new day.

I walked down the stairs to Eddie's casino. The man himself was drinking Scotch at the end of the bar. I sidled up next to him and took a seat. "Eddie, what's good?"

He smiled. "Money comes and money goes, but if you're breathing, it's all good."

"I'll drink to that." Eddie raised an eyebrow, and I shook my head. "Not literally. Grover came to see me this morning."

"He's up early."

"Nah. Up late. Like you."

Eddie smiled, flashing a gold tooth. "My wife used to get on my case about that. 'You work all night,' she'd say. 'We never see each other. We're like ships passing in the night.' That's what she actually said. 'Ships passing in the night.'"

Vivian set a glass of club soda in front of me. I watched it bubble and then I took a sip. "How'd you resolve it?"

"Resolve what?"

"The problems with your wife. The ships passing. How'd you work it out?"

Eddie shrugged. "I told her it was shift work, like any other. What did Grover want?"

"He wants to kill Sammy DiAngelo."

Eddie put down his drink and scanned the room. "Jesus, Jack. Take an ad out in the paper, why doncha?"

"So you think it'd be a bad idea."

"You know my motto, Jack. Avoid trouble if you can."

"And if you can't?"

The big man nodded slowly. "That's the sad, unfortunate thing about this world of ours, isn't it? Sometimes trouble can't be avoided." He stared at me. "In that case, you run toward it, swinging, and you hope for the best." He sat back. "Marcus came by earlier, looking for you."

"He okay?"

Eddie stood up. "Why don't you ask him yourself? He's in my office."

"Marcus."

"Jack." Marcus looked genuinely happy to see me. He gave me a hearty handshake. "Lookin' sharp, my man."

"Everything okay?"

77

"Far as I know." He rubbed his eyebrow with his pointer finger and cleared his throat. "I heard from Beatrice yesterday."

"Yeah? How's she doing?"

"She's wondering if she has a job."

I glanced over at the closed office door. "Marcus, am I a fucking idiot?"

"What?"

"Because I must be a fucking idiot to have thought I could pull this off."

"This ..."

"This. Palace Security. Going legit. The whole bit."

Marcus looked down at Eddie's carpet. It was from Afghanistan. There were pictures of Kalashnikovs and AK-47s woven into the design. "So that's it, then."

I shook my head. "I didn't say that." I grinned. "We're not licked yet."

There was a knock on the door. Eddie opened it up and smiled. "Dig me, knocking on the door of my own office." He looked over at Marcus. "Freshen your drink?"

Marcus's glass of Scotch looked untouched. "No thanks, I'm good."

Eddie looked over at me. "I just got a call from my man at the precinct. That licence plate you wanted came back." He grinned, holding up a slip of paper. "It wasn't stolen. Can you believe that? Those dumb shits used their own truck."

I took the paper from Eddie, unfolded it, and read. Then I looked up. "Well," I said, "looks like we're going for a drive in the country."

Marcus shifted, uncomfortable. "Jack, I, ah —"

"Marcus, I think you've got some stuff to do around the city. Right?"

He looked relieved. "Yeah. Thanks, Jack. Good luck."

Luck was all well and good, but what I needed was muscle. Eddie, Vin, and Eddie's guy Roger drove with me. We took one of Eddie's cars. I had never seen it before, and I wagered that after today, I would never see it again. No doubt Eddie's name was nowhere near the registration. Unlike the man we were driving to see. His John Hancock was on the red Chevy's registration, plain as day. Quentin O'Banion. I had never heard of him, but I was guessing he had heard of me.

Vin twisted the radio dial until he landed on Gloria Gaynor. She was belting out "I Will Survive." Roger shook his head. "Uh-uh, man. Cool it with that disco shit."

Vin cocked his head. "What? What have you got against disco?"

"It's ..."

"Too gay?"

"No. C'mon, Vin —"

"Too Black?"

"No! It's ... you know. Disco sucks."

"It's dance music, Roger. What's wrong with dancing?"

"Nothing. It's just ... you know. That disco shit. It's fake. It's corny."

"You're thinking about the disco fad. You have to think about disco in two different ways. There was the real underground dance music, like what David Mancuso played at the Loft and Larry Levan played at the Paradise Garage, and then there was the disco fad that swept the world after *Saturday Night Fever* came out. When every chophouse in the city added turntables and called itself a discotheque. That shit might've been fake and corny, but the real shit, the real disco, that shit is pure solid gold."

Roger held up his hands. "All right, all right." Vin leaned forward and turned the music up.

Eddie glanced at me in the rear-view mirror and grinned. "You comfortable back there?"

I smiled back. "Just chillin', learnin' about disco."

"Take it up with Vin another time. We're here."

Quentin O'Banion's house was nothing to write home about. It was a quiet bungalow on a quiet street just outside of Orangeville. We circled the neighbourhood and didn't see anything out of the ordinary, so we came back and parked across the street. Then Eddie and I walked up the driveway looking like the world's worst missionaries. *Excuse me, sir, have you heard the Good News?* I knocked on the door, then I knocked again. We weren't bringing Quentin any good news.

A man opened the door and stood there, blinking. He was in his midsixties, or possibly early seventies. He was wearing a white tank top and a pair of brown-and-white-striped pyjama pants. "Whatever you're selling, I don't want any." He started to close the door.

"Quentin O'Banion?" I made my voice deep and forceful. All official-like. That made Mr. O'Banion pause.

"Yes?"

"May we come in for a minute, sir?"

"What's this about?"

"It's about your truck, sir."

"Oh, Jesus. Did that idiot crash it again?" The old man took a step back so we could pass through the doorway and step into the living room. He closed the door after us. "Is he okay?"

"Sir?"

"My nephew. He crashed again, right? Is he okay?"

"He's fine. He borrowed your truck?"

"He's been driving it all summer. Has a job in town at the hardware store. He's been using my truck to get from point A to point B."

"What's your nephew's name?"

"Mike. Mike Travis."

Eddie stepped forward. "Where can we find Mr. Travis? We just need to ask him a few questions."

"He lives with my sister — 305 Mockingbird Way. You sure he's okay?"

"Thank you for your time, sir."

Outside, the sun was shining. I had a friend once whose mother was visiting from Laos. She had never experienced a cold winter. She came to Toronto in December, and pretty much the whole month was cold, dark, and grey. Then one day the skies were blue and the sun was shining, and my friend's mother ran outside, thinking that the sunshine meant it was warm weather at last. She was so surprised to find out that the sun could shine and yet the world could still be plenty cold.

Eddie and I got back into the car. "You think he'll call ahead? Tip off the nephew?" he said.

"Yeah, probably."

"He's going to be in the wind."

"Maybe. Maybe not. O'Banion thought we were cops."

"It's that great cop voice of yours." Eddie grinned. "Gets 'em every time."

I shrugged. "Not every time. This time, yes."

"You think it'll work on the nephew?"

"Only one way to find out."

CHAPTER 15

The house at 305 Mockingbird Way had fallen on hard times. There was a brown pickup truck without tires up on blocks on the driveway. Weeds poked up from cracks in the walkway leading up to the house. A miniature wishing well was half-hidden by overgrown grass. I peered in the dirty window and looked into the living room. It was messy, but that wasn't a crime. Eddie and I stepped onto the front porch and I knocked on the door. Instantly, a dog started to bark.

After about a minute a young man opened the door. He was holding a tiny snarling dog in his arms. "Yeah? What do you want?"

"Mike Travis?"

"Yeah?"

"Is your mother at home, Mike?"

"She's at work. At the hospital. What is this?"

"May we come in?"

Mike's brow was furrowed like he knew something was wrong, but he couldn't figure out what. He stepped aside, and Eddie and I walked into the house. There was a smell of cabbage and the faint scent of dog pee. "You alone in the house?"

"Just me and Polly here. What's this about my mom? Is she okay?"

"Put Polly in the bedroom. Then we'll talk."

Eddie followed Mike to the bedroom. Mike put Polly inside and closed the door. The little dog yapped, pleading to be let out.

"What's this about?" he said.

"Well, it's about you firebombing my trailer, Mike."

The man's eyes went wide. He turned and ran for the kitchen. Eddie tripped him and Big Mike went sprawling. Eddie reached down and hauled him to his feet. I hit him once, twice, three times. Blood trickled from Mike's mouth. My hand stung. "Why did you do it, Mike?"

"I didn't know it was your trailer."

"What's that? I didn't quite hear you."

"I didn't know it was your trailer! I met this guy in a bar. He said he wanted to scare somebody. Someone owed him some money and he wanted to scare them into paying up. That's what he told me."

"He lied to you. How much did he pay you?"

"Five grand. Look, I'm sorry. I needed the money."

"He pay you before or after?"

"After. I met him in a motel room out on Highway 10." Mike was shaking now. "Please. I'm sorry. Don't kill me. Please."

"Who else was in the truck with you?"

"A buddy of mine. Please. He doesn't know anything."

Eddie loomed over him. "We need a name."

I shook my head. "No."

"No?" Eddie looked at me, confused.

I stared at Mike. "The guy at the bar. What did he look like?"

"I don't know, man. I was pretty drunk."

"Try to remember," Eddie hissed into Mike's ear.

"He, uh, had dark hair. Late thirties, maybe early forties. He was wearing a suit. That I remember because he looked way out of place. He had the suit on at the motel, too."

"Could you contact him again?"

Mike shook his head. "He said to meet him at the motel when the job was done. I went, got my money, and that was that."

"Where's the money now?"

"It's gone. I spent it."

Eddie looked like he wanted to throw Big Mike through a wall. I wrote out a phone number on a piece of paper and handed it to Mike. "If he contacts you again, call this number."

"I will. But I don't think he'll call."

"I know. But if he does, you let me know."

The cold air kissed my skinned knuckles. Eddie breathed deep and exhaled a huge steamy puff. "Another dead end."

"We know a few more things."

"The man in the suit. You think he's mobbed up?"

"Either that or someone's pointing the blame that way."

Eddie cocked his head back at the house. "We should've ended that little punk."

"It was a trailer, Eddie. Is a trailer worth a human life?"

"It's the principle of the thing," he grumbled.

"He's just a dumb kid who got drunk and did something dumb. We've all been there."

"You're in a forgiving mood."

I swung open the car door. "Tell that to Suzanne. She thinks I haven't changed."

The drive back to the city was uneventful. We stopped at a roadside produce stand and Eddie bought a few fruit pies for his casino staff. There were no more fights about the radio. Eddie found the jazz station and left it there.

Roger sat in the back holding the pies. "Vin and I didn't even get out of the car."

Eddie nodded. "That's how it goes sometimes."

"I'm just saying, why bring us all the way out here —"

"I said, that's how it goes sometimes."

I turned back to Roger. "We might've needed you. But as it turned out, we didn't."

Vin leaned forward. "So the guy wasn't the guy?"

"Oh, the guy was the guy, all right. We found the guy who burned the trailer." I held up my bruised hand. "We had a little chat about it. Turns out he was just the hired help."

"So now what?"

Eddie frowned. "We're going home. Roger, don't drop those pies, now."

CHAPTER 16

The pies were good. Eddie had bought apple, strawberry, and cherry. I had a slice of apple and washed it down with a big glass of club soda. Pie and club soda didn't exactly mix but what the hell. I was feeling good. I had found one of the men who burned down my trailer. I didn't know who had hired him, and maybe I never would, but it still felt like closure. That was a bullshit word, "closure." It made more sense in Hallmark movies than it did in real life. One door closes, another opens, and on and on until the big dirt nap. Me, I was still smiling, I was eating pie, I was alive.

Vin came up to me. He was smiling, too. "There's a woman upstairs who wants to see you."

I forked the last of the pie into my mouth, wiped my mouth with a paper napkin (sorry, trees), and stood up. "Did she give you a name?"

"She did." Eddie smiled. "It's Suzanne."

I took the stairs two at a time, heading for Eddie's restaurant on the ground floor. Suzanne was there at a table near the front window. The sun was pouring in. She looked like she was glowing. There were two platters of food in front of her. She saw me and smiled. "You're just in time for lunch."

I pulled up a chair. "I could eat." Dessert first, then lunch. Stay out all night and sleep during the day. My life was like a photographic negative. Everything in reverse.

"How's the security business?"

"I won't lie. It's slow. Having my trailer burned down was a real setback."

"But you can get a new trailer."

"I could." Back to the grind. Hustling for clients. Keeping the employees happy. Working out payroll. Filing taxes. All that mundane day-to-day business that kept the whole ball of wax rolling. At least I didn't have to apply for another business license. The one I had didn't expire for another two and a half years.

Suzanne stared at me. "You don't look happy."

"No?"

She sipped her drink. "As soon as I said you could get another trailer, you flinched. As if I'd just thwacked your nipples or something."

"Thwacked my nipples?"

"Forget it." She leaned in closer. "Do you really want your own security company?"

"I thought I did. I thought my skills would carry over, you know, from the nighttime world into the light."

"And now?"

"It's a whole lot of hassle."

"That's why they call it work."

"What are you doing these days?"

"I got another bartending gig. It's an old punk bar in Kensington Market. Great music, but the tips are shit." Suzanne reached over and took my hand. She lightly brushed her thumb over my skinned knuckles.

"I, uh, had a disagreement."

She took her hand away. "Forget it, Jack. You don't owe me an explanation."

"Is everything okay?"

"You tell me."

"There's some guys that want to kill me. You know — same as it ever was."

"You sound almost happy about that." She looked at me sideways. "What would you do without someone to fight?"

"I'd sleep. I haven't had a good night's sleep in I don't know how long." I did know, actually. It was about ten years, when Suzanne and I were together. We had made love and then fallen asleep with our limbs entwined, her naked body on top of mine, our chests rising and falling together.

"Thing is, Jack, you're a fighter. You'll always want to fight."

I stared at her. Those big dark eyes, those full, round lips. "Maybe you're right. Maybe the trick is to channel that fighting spirit into something productive. Fight city hall, that sort of thing. Stand up for the little guy. Go after corporations poisoning people's well water."

She smiled. "You mean like an investigator for a law firm?"

"Yeah, maybe." I popped some deep-fried shrimp into my mouth. "I don't know what I mean."

She took my hand again. "You once told me you wanted to retire. Put all the fighting behind you and move out to a little cabin in the woods. Remember?"

"There'd be a garden. And chickens for fresh eggs." In this fantasy, I wasn't alone. Suzanne was there, too, standing on the porch in a long dress with a pitcher of lemonade in her hand.

Her eyes twinkled. "I remember. I'd be lying if I said I haven't thought about that cabin over the past ten years. I would go there sometimes, in my mind. Especially when Steve got sick."

"Your man."

"That's right. Sometimes when I was in the hospital with him, I would close my eyes and I'd be in that cabin. Your cabin. You'd be there, too. You'd hold me and tell me everything would be all right. And even though I knew it wasn't true, I liked hearing it. I liked hearing it from you." She laughed. "It sounds corny, doesn't it?"

"No. Not at all. We all take comfort where we can find it."

She looked me right in the eyes. "Have you really quit drinking?"

"Yes. I still think about it, though. All the time." I looked away. "It's hard to face the world sober."

She smiled gently. "Sobriety is a gift, Jack." She passed me a platter. "More shrimp?"

We sat and ate with the sun streaming in.

CHAPTER 17

Retirement. More and more, it was looking like a great option. The problem was, I didn't have the cash. Maybe Suzanne was right and I would always be a fighter. Still, that didn't mean I couldn't cool my heels for a bit on a porch or a beach. The world was the world; there would always be another injustice to fight. But even the heavyweight champion of the world gets to kick back every now and then.

So, then, how to scrape up the cash? Get my security company up and running again? Build it up, sell it off. It sounded impossible, yet shit like that happened every day. Trouble was, it would take years. Between now and then, I might be found floating belly-up in the lake with my throat slit from ear to ear. My problems would be over, but it wasn't much of a retirement plan.

My couch creaked as I leaned forward. I stared at the empty space on my desk where my plant had been. I got up, picked up one of Eddie's boxes of lollipops, and set it on the desk. Damn, I missed that plant. It wasn't just the plant but everything it had represented. Green shoots poking up from the dirt. A fresh start, a new life. I stared at the box of lollipops. It wasn't doing it for me. "Time to get a new plant," I muttered.

I was putting on my jacket to head out to the plant store when my phone rang. I fished it from my pocket and stared at the screen. I didn't recognize the number.

"Hello?"

"Is this Mr. Palace?" A man's voice, buttery and sweet. Whoever it was had said only four words, and already I didn't trust him at all.

"Who's asking?"

"I'm a friend of a friend. I've got someone here who wants to say hello."

There was a brief thumping and crackling as the phone got shifted around.

"Jack!"

"Marcus?"

"I'm sorry, Jack. They made me give them your number."

"Who's got you? Hello? Hello?" I pressed the phone tight against my ear in frustration. "Marcus!"

The phone crackled. The buttery voice was back. "Your friend Marcus is fine, for now. But you know how dangerous winter can be. One slip, one fall, and things could change in an instant."

My knuckles turned white as I squeezed the phone. "You listen to me and you listen carefully. If you hurt that man, I will kill you. Do you understand?"

"No one wants that. I'd like to meet with you, Mr. Palace. The Exhibition grounds, down by the lake. The

Dufferin Gate. This evening. Shall we say around 7:00 p.m.? Until then."

The phone went dead in my hand. *Marcus. Oh, fuck, Marcus. What did I drag you into?*

Eddie paced across the Afghan carpet in his office. From the other side of the door came a loud cheer as some lucky sucker won it big. Eddie paused his pacing, rustled through his desk drawer, and pulled out a lollipop. He stripped off the cellophane and then he realized he already had one in his mouth. He cursed and tossed the lollipop to the floor. "Fuck this, Jack. I want a fucking smoke."

"You want a smoke, I want a drink, but neither of those things is going to help get Marcus back."

"You know what I think."

"Yeah, I know what you think. You think it's a fucking set-up."

"Well, isn't it?"

"Yeah, probably. But I've got to go."

"You're not going alone. Vin, Roger — fuck it, let's bring everybody. We'll pile into cars, we'll get some machine guns, and when that motherfucker shows his fucking face we'll light the place up like Christmas."

I nodded slowly. "You know I appreciate the sentiment. But if we do that —"

"Yeah, yeah. I know." Eddie ran his hand through his greying hair. "If we do that, Marcus is as good as dead. I'm serious, though, Jack. You're not going alone."

"Weird thing is, the guy didn't say anything about coming alone."

"He knows you're not calling the cops." Eddie popped the lollipop out of his mouth and stared at it. "He's not worried about you bringing an army because he's got an army, too."

I nodded again. "That's my take on it. Marcus isn't going to be anywhere near Exhibition Place tonight." It made me sick thinking of Marcus trapped in some dingy room somewhere. Had they hurt him? My fists tightened at my sides.

I was walking into a trap. I felt like I was in a giant's fist and the giant was squeezing slowly, choking all the air out of my lungs. I couldn't let Marcus die.

Eddie rallied the troops. I went up to my office and strapped on my knives. One around my ankle, one on my lower arm, one around my chest underneath my jacket. If I had to go down, I would go down fighting. I'd known this since I was nineteen, known it with a clarity that was almost frightening: I was going to die fighting. It was only a matter of time.

Of course, as my buddy The Chief used to say, ain't nobody have a crystal ball. Would I die tonight? Maybe I'd step off the curb at the wrong time and place and get flattened by a bus. Maybe the bus wouldn't kill me, but it would send me to the hospital, hooked up delirious and dreaming to a dozen beeping machines. Maybe I'd see that fabled tunnel of light. And at the end of the tunnel, my mother, actually smiling, finally at peace.

I wanted to live. Life was cold and it was hard, but it was worth fighting for. I zipped my jacket up over the knives and looked over at the box of lollipops on my desk. I'd get another plant, I would. Just not tonight.

The number one rule for meetings like this was to always get there early. Patrol the perimeter, check for traps. Maybe the other guys had an army, and maybe that army was lying in wait. To get the drop on someone, you had to surprise them. You had to get there first.

Down in the casino, Eddie and the boys were strapping up. I don't like guns, but like any tool, there are times when they are necessary. Still, bullets are harsh and unfeeling. They come out of the gun and that's it, there's no taking it back. Innocent people get killed in crossfires daily, all around the world.

Eddie stared at me grimly. "You ready?" I glanced over at the clock on Eddie's office wall. It was 4:00 p.m. It would take us about half an hour to get down to the Dufferin Gate from Chinatown, depending on traffic. We'd be two and a half hours early. I wasn't about to sit on a bench by the arch of the gate for that long. We'd scope out the scene and then set up camp and wait. I glanced over at Eddie's desk. I knew there was a bottle of high-end Scotch in there, deep in a drawer. I wanted a shot or two for luck. Just a little drink, something to warm the ol' bones as we patrolled through the snow.

I tilted my head toward the desk. "You still got a bottle in there?"

Eddie stared at me. "You know I do."

"Break it out."

Eddie didn't say anything. He just kept staring at me. I stared back, frowning. "Fine. Fuck it. Forget about it."

"Better to go in with a clear head."

I'd thought it would be better to go in a little bit warm, a little bit loose, but whatever, I'd been wrong before. Eddie, Roger, Vin and I trooped out.

Roger glanced sideways at Vin. "I get to pick the music this time."

Vin blinked. "What?"

"You got to pick the music last time. It's my turn."

Eddie scowled. "Are you three years old? 'My turn.' Fuck that. A man's life is on the line and you want to play disc jockey? Get your head outta your ass."

Roger stared down at the ground. "Sorry. My bad."

We stepped out into the alley. A cold wind swirled snow. Eddie popped the collar of his coat and turned to us. "We'll take two cars. Jack's with me. Roger and Vin, you take the Camry."

Our boots stamped through the snow. Car doors opened and car doors slammed closed. Eddie didn't turn on the radio and neither did I. He fired up the engine of his Lexus. Roger pulled the Camry into formation behind us. Together, we all headed for the Ex.

CHAPTER 18

The Dufferin Gate had been torn down and rebuilt several times since it was first built in 1895. The current gate had been built after the old one was torn down in 1959, to make room for the Gardiner Expressway. The new gate didn't even look like a gate. It looked like a miniature version of the St. Louis Gateway Arch, although the Gateway Arch wasn't completed until 1965, which meant that the Dufferin Gate had come first.

Eddie pulled into a parking lot near the Dufferin Gate and left the motor running. He and I both scanned the parking lot. Vast domed roofs rose up before us, Canadian flags snap-crackling in the cold November breeze.

"See anything?"

I shook my head. "You?"

"Nothing out of the ordinary." Eddie tilted his head back toward the arch. "I got a good view from here. Vin and Roger will set up camp on the other side. You go and do your thing. If you need help, I'll come running."

Chances were that if I needed help, I'd be dead long before Eddie or Roger or Vin arrived. But it gave me a bit of comfort knowing that my death would be avenged and my bleeding body scooped up from the ground. Eddie and the gang could lay me out on the casino bar and have a nice little wake. A dead man on the bar wasn't exactly good for business, but Eddie could afford to shut down for a few hours.

"You okay?" Eddie said.

"Yeah. Just thinking." I grinned. "If I die, throw a nice wake, okay?"

"How 'bout you just don't fucking die?"

Hours went by. We didn't talk much. Now and then Eddie turned on the engine to warm up the car.

Right around 7:00 p.m. I turned to him and smiled. "All right, fuck it. Here I go."

I stepped out into the darkness. That was one thing I hated about the wintertime. The sun set so damn early. At least there still was some sun during the day. If you went far enough north, it was pitch black for months at a time. I didn't know how anyone could live like that, but if there was one thing I'd learned over the years, it was that human beings were pretty damn resilient.

The arch was lit up against the night. The pavilions were, too, giving the Exhibition grounds a kind of fairy tale quality. As if any minute a knight in shining armour would come charging past, chasing a fire-breathing dragon.

I walked through the arch and found a bench. I stood there waiting.

I didn't have to wait long. A man in a grey flannel suit and a long trench coat approached from the darkness. He was wearing a fedora, as if he were a salesman from the 1950s. I watched him come closer. He was watching me watch him. I nodded slightly. The man nodded back.

"Mr. Palace. Thanks for coming."

"And you are?"

"My name isn't important, but you can call me Richard." The man sat down on the bench. "Join me, won't you?"

I sat down, too. "Now that we're all chummy with the first names, Richard, why don't you tell me where I can find Marcus."

"He's safe, I assure you." The man's buttery voice was the same as the voice on the phone. His face looked buttery, too. Shiny as if coated with oil. "He's an innocent in all of this. We didn't want to scoop him up, but it was necessary to get your attention."

"Well, you've got it. What the fuck do you want?"

"You do have a reputation for vulgarity, Mr. Palace. I imagine that in the circles you run in, that vulgarity has served you well."

"Cut the crap. I'll ask you again: what the fuck do you want?"

The man's eyebrows shot up. "There's a significant price on your head. You're aware of this, no doubt."

"Is that why you're here?"

"No, no. I'm not motivated by money. At least, not entirely." The man smiled. "I am curious by nature, and I'm afraid that my curiosity has gotten the best of me." He leaned closer. He smelled like cinnamon and burnt toast. "You tell me what I want to know, and I will tell you where to find your friend Marcus, unharmed as promised." He pulled a lavender-coloured handkerchief from his pocket and wiped his lips. There was something unsettlingly obscene about the gesture. "Who killed Freddy?"

"Word is, I did."

"In this case, I believe that the 'word,' as you say, is wrong." The man stared at me, his face suddenly hard. "Please don't ask me to repeat myself."

"I don't know."

The man sighed. "You may be good at many things, Mr. Palace, but lying is not one of them. And so, I shall be forced to repeat myself after all. Who killed Freddy?"

"I'm telling you, I don't know."

"We believe it was a man called Grover. Furthermore, I believe you know this."

"Who are you working for?"

"I'll ask the questions, if you don't mind. Who killed Tommy?"

"Who?"

"Now you're just insulting my intelligence. Tommy, the man who saved your life in jail. His body was never found, but he is undoubtedly dead. Once again, fingers point in your direction."

"Tommy saved my life. I saved his twice. I told him to retire." I shrugged. "Maybe he did."

"We believe this man Grover had something to do with Tommy's disappearance. Grover — he is an associate of yours, is he not?"

"I know him."

The man smiled again. Snow drifted down past the lights of the arch. "That is the truest thing you've said yet. The price on your head, Mr. Palace. Surely it's an inconvenience to you."

"The cost of doing business."

"Ah, but it depends on the business, doesn't it?" He shot me a smirk. "Palace Security. That's a noble effort on your part, Jack. I imagine you're eager to get back to it."

"Tell me where Marcus is."

"He works for you, doesn't he? A security guard."

I didn't say anything. What was the point? This man Richard, or whoever he was, seemed to know it all already. "We'd like to hire you, Mr. Palace."

"Who's 'we'?"

"I said, I'll ask the questions." He stood up. "Remove your associate Grover from the picture, and the price on your head goes away."

"What?"

"You heard what I said."

I rose to my feet. The snow kept falling. Light, soft flakes. "You're just a stranger. Some man off the street."

Richard nodded. "This is true. So, then, a token of my good faith." He checked his watch. "As soon as I walk away and make a call, you will find your friend Marcus back at Eddie's casino. He will be unharmed, as promised. We need Grover dead, Mr. Palace. I hate to phrase this so bluntly, but it's either him or you. Decide quickly, please. You have forty-eight hours."

He turned, tugged on the brim of his fedora, and headed out into the snow. With one gesture I could bring in Vin and Roger and Eddie, but where would that lead?

No doubt Richard had his own troops waiting in the wings. There would be blood, and then Marcus would be as good as dead.

I watched the man walk away, then I turned and walked slowly back to Eddie's waiting car.

CHAPTER 19

Marcus was alive and well, waiting for us at the casino just as Richard had promised. We embraced and I hugged him tight, tight, tight. I broke the embrace and stared at him. "Are you okay?"

He nodded. "Little shaken up, is all." He smiled sheepishly. "I'd take a drink, if anyone's offering."

Eddie circled his finger in the air. "Drinks all around. Jack, you want a Coke?"

I wanted whisky and lots of it. "Club soda."

Eddie clapped me on the back. "Good man." He pressed a glass of Scotch into Marcus's hand. "Glad to have you back."

"It's good to be back."

Eddie jerked his thumb over his shoulder. "You guys want to talk, you can use my office."

Marcus and I walked past the poker tables. A woman in a silver sequined top pushed in two stacks of chips. "All in." The man sitting across from her folded, slapping his cards against the table in disgust. The woman smiled as the dealer pushed the chips her way.

As soon as Eddie's office door was closed, Marcus collapsed onto a leather chair with a great shuddering exhale. "I won't lie, I was scared fucking shitless."

"Tell me what happened."

"I was on my way to a friend's house. This van pulled up and the back door slid open. Two guys jumped out, pulled me in, and the van took off." He looked up at me. "I tried to fight them, Jack. I tried to use what you taught me, but it all happened so fast."

"No one's blaming you, Marcus."

"They hit me in the stomach and I couldn't breathe. I just doubled up there on the van floor." He blinked. "It was one of those white panel vans. Totally nondescript."

"And the guys?"

"They were white. One of them was wearing a dark-blue track suit with white piping on the legs. The other one had on jeans and a dark-grey sweater. One of them didn't look like anything special. The other guy looked kind of misshapen, like his face had this lumpy look, as if he was made out of clay and the person making him had stopped just before they were done. They took me to a basement apartment. I'm not sure where. They tied me to a chair. I tried to resist them, I swear."

"It's okay. It's not your fault."

"They didn't say anything. That was the scary part. No demands or anything." Marcus took another deep, shuddering breath. "I thought I was going to die."

"You didn't, though. You're alive."

"Yeah." He ducked his head and stared at the floor.

"I can't do this, Jack. I thought I could, but I can't." He looked up. "I'm leaving tomorrow. I'm going to stay with my family in Halifax, get my head straight."

"I understand."

"Look, I feel bad about running out on you. Leaving the company and everything."

"It's okay. Go. Spend time with your family."

"I'm sorry. I hate myself for running."

"Don't do that. Hating yourself isn't the way forward. You're not running from something, you're running to something. That's a big difference."

He looked at me with his big brown eyes. "You think I'm a coward, Jack?"

"No. Not at all. I think you're smart. You gotta know when to lay down your cards and walk away." I reached down and gave his shoulder a pat. "I'm going to find those guys, Marcus. They're not going to bother you again."

Together, we left the office. The casino was in full swing. The woman in the sequined top raked in another pot. She reminded me a bit of Cassandra but only a bit.

Eddie and I watched Marcus leave the casino. He looked ashamed, like a whipped dog. I hoped Halifax would get his head straight. It wasn't his fault he'd gotten jumped, it was mine.

Eddie glanced over at me. "Don't blame yourself."

"Goddamn, Eddie. You a mind reader now?"

He grinned. "I know you, that's all. I know what you're thinking. You're thinking, if Marcus had never met you, he wouldn't have gotten jumped. Think about it, though. If Marcus never met you, he'd still be slinging coke for Melody. Right?"

"Maybe."

"No maybes about it. Either Melody would've betrayed him, or he would've been arrested, or a rival dealer would've put a bullet in his head. You put him on the path to the straight and narrow."

"No, maybe I showed him the path, but he was the one who decided to walk down it."

"Well, there you go." Eddie smiled. "Maybe when he gets settled, you can write him a glowing letter of recommendation. Lots of other security companies out there. Maybe he can get a job kicking rowdy teens out of some Halifax mall." He clapped me on the back. "Come on, let's get a drink."

We sat down at the bar. Vin walked up to us holding a printout. He slapped it onto the bar. "Bingo bango, there he is."

I stared at the picture on the paper. It was Richard, fedora and all. Vin smiled. "I got a bunch of different angles, but that's the best one."

"Good job." I slid the paper toward Eddie. "Get your cop to run this through the system. They must have some facial recognition software down at the station, right?"

"Yeah, probably."

"Good. Let's see what comes up. In the meantime, Vin and I will take copies around and see if anyone recognizes this smooth-taking prick." I frowned. "I hated the way he talked. So damn buttery and fake." What did the man really sound like, without all the bullshit?

Eddie looked down at the picture again. "Might be tough, Jack. He looks like a million other people."

"Not everyone can have a birthmark and a duelling scar. We'll ask around and maybe we'll get lucky." I sipped my club soda.

"Yeah, maybe. You heard from Grover recently?"

"Not a thing. All quiet on the Western Front."

"Whoever Mr. Butterface is, he wants me to kill Grover."

Eddie blinked. "That's gonna be tricky."

"I'm not going to do it, Eddie."

"Yeah. On the other hand, Grover's tried to kill you before."

I drained the last of my drink. "We worked all that out. Butterface is connected to the mob somehow. He knows a lot of shit about Tommy and Freddy. Sounds like they want to put the weight on Grover and let me skate."

"You really think they'll let you skate?"

"Nope. That's what Butterface wants me to think. That if I kill Grover, the mob is satisfied, and my life goes back to normal, whatever that is."

"You know it won't work like that."

"Oh, hell, no. I kill Grover and the next thing that happens is I get an ice pick in the back of the throat."

"An ice pick?"

"Or a knife or a bullet. Either way, I'm just as dead."

"So you're not going to kill him."

I stared down at my empty glass. "What I'm looking for here, Eddie, is what Buddhists call the Middle Way." I tapped my finger against Mr. Butterface's picture. "We find out who this prick is, and suddenly I've got a lot more options."

Eddie nodded and picked up the picture. "I'm on it."

CHAPTER 20

Nobody knew shit. Vin and I pounded the pavement all night long, ducking into bars, clubs, and restaurants. We went into private homes and apartments. We showed people Mr. Butterface's picture and described his creepy bullshit voice. Everywhere we went, it was the same old story. Nobody knew him, nobody saw him, nobody had ever heard of him before. Despite having talked to the man personally, I was starting to suspect he didn't exist.

Then we got lucky. Paula, a bartender at the Pearl, this after-hours joint above a fabric store on Queen West, took one look at Mr. Butterface's picture and shuddered. The joint wasn't open yet — it would start swinging right around 3:00 a.m., a little after last call in the clubs — but Paula still looked around to make sure no one could hear her. "Yeah, I know him," she said in a soft, quiet voice. "He had a thing with one of my bartenders. Nadine. You know her, Jack. Has all the flower tattoos up and down her arms and legs."

I nodded. Paula kept talking. "It must've been, I don't know, probably about three months back. Before it started getting cold. This guy" — she jabbed her finger at Mr. Butterface's picture — "was in here with another guy. Big guy with his face all rubbery, like he was wearing a mask."

"Was he?"

"Was he what?"

"Was he wearing a mask?"

Paula shook her head. "No, it was the dude's real face. It was just … lumpy, you know? As if his face was made of dough."

"Or clay?"

"Yeah, sure, clay. So Clayface was just sitting there looking all sour and ignoring the drink in his hand. Your guy here, he was beaming like he'd just won the lottery. Had a real weird twinkle in his eyes, you know? And he was sweet-talking Nadine something fierce. I remember because orders were getting backed up at the bar. I had to walk over and tell her to get her head back in the game. This guy kissed her hand before she left, made her giggle. I knew he had her hooked, and I wasn't wrong. Right around five-thirty, he and Nadine left together. Clayface stayed for another twenty minutes or so, making me all nervous. Not doing anything, you know, just sitting there giving me the heebie-jeebies. I was working up my nerve to tell him to leave, that we were shutting the place for the morning, when he stood up and left on his own. I don't mind telling you I breathed a sigh of relief."

Paula stared down at the picture. "The next night, Nadine didn't come into work. An hour went by and

I still hadn't heard from her, so I gave her a call. Her phone went right to voice mail. Another hour, still no Nadine. Again the phone went right to voice mail. I had a feeling something was wrong, like really wrong, so I got Charles the bouncer to drive me to Nadine's place. I had a key, so I let myself in. The first thing I heard was groaning. I ran to the bedroom — which maybe wasn't the smartest thing I could've done, but you know me, Jack. I didn't even think of calling the cops. Nadine was naked, sprawled out on the bed, her left arm and her left leg dangling over the floor. There was blood everywhere. She ..." Paula looked away, then back at me. "She'd been beaten, Jack. Badly. Her whole face was red and raw. She'd been cut, too. And burned. If I hadn't gotten there when I did, I'm sure that girl would've died."

I held up the picture. "And you're sure this is the guy who did it?"

Paula nodded. "I'm sure." She pushed the picture away. "Put that thing away, will you? I don't want anything to do with it."

I nodded. "You never said a word."

"That's right. Keep me out of it."

"Is Nadine working tonight?"

"She is. She ... she's changed, Jack. Before, she was real outgoing, you know? Bubbly. Now she doesn't trust anyone. Keeps to herself. I have to remind her to smile at the customers." Paula shrugged. "She's a good bartender, though. Works hard. After what happened, I can't bear to let her go."

"Would she talk to me?"

"Maybe. Maybe not. Like I said, she doesn't trust anyone. Especially not men."

I folded the picture away and stood up. "I'll be back." I turned to go and then I turned back toward Paula. "Oh, just one more thing. You seen Grover around?"

"Last time that little shit was here, he stole a bottle of whisky. The good stuff, too."

"When was that?"

"About a month ago. If you see him, tell him to get fucked."

I met up with Vin at Suzanne's old bar. I walked in and Vin jerked his thumb at the bartender. The one with the tattoos and the floppy hair was working the pumps. "He doesn't know anything. And I don't just mean about Mr. Butterface. That guy doesn't know anything about anything."

"C'mon, Vin. Be nice." I sat down and scanned the room. No Grover, no Suzanne. "I got a hit. Turns out our man is a sadistic little fuckhead. You know Nadine over at the Pearl? He hurt her. He hurt her real bad."

Vin frowned. "I like Nadine."

"Mr. Butterface beat her to a pulp. Cut her and burned her. I don't want to bother her, but I need to go back to the Pearl tonight and talk to her."

"You want me to come with you?"

"No. She doesn't like men anymore. Two men looming over her asking about the time she almost got killed would be too much."

"You think she'll talk to you?"

"No. But I have to try."

———

111

Turns out I was right. Nadine didn't want to tell me shit. As soon as I showed her the picture, she clammed right up. I couldn't blame her. I was hoping she would know his name, his occupation, some scrap of information that would eventually lead me to his door. Instead I got a whole lot of nothing. It was sad, the way her smile had been wiped from her face. I remembered her as happy, outgoing, laughing as she mixed the drinks. That Nadine was gone, maybe forever. And I was willing to bet she hadn't been the first. Butterface or Richard or whatever the fuck his real name was had done this to other women. This and maybe worse.

"Sorry, Jack," Paula said as I was leaving.

I shook my head. "Don't be. I'm sorry to bother her."

"I could ask around if you want."

"No. Keep your mouth shut. Keep out of it. Remember, I was never here."

There was one other person I could ask about Butterface. One person who might have some glimmering of understanding as to what this guy was all about. And that person was Grover, the man I was supposed to kill.

CHAPTER 21

Even at the best of times, Grover was like a ghost. In the summer he lived on his boat, and whenever he didn't like the way the wind was blowing, he would simply hoist anchor and haul ass to sunnier climes. In the winter he usually flew south like a bird. Maybe that was where he was now, cooling his heels on a beach, a frozen daiquiri in his hand. No one had seen him. The ghost had ghosted.

I sat in my office surrounded by Eddie's boxes. I picked the box of lollipops up off my desk and set it on the floor. Then I picked up the jade plant I'd bought and set it on the desk near the window. There was no natural light this late at night, but maybe the plant would appreciate the neon flash of Chinatown. I went to the bathroom and poured lukewarm water into a glass. Then I walked over and watered the plant. "Welcome to your new home, Plant." I stared down at it. It didn't look happy. "Don't look like that. It's not so bad."

There was a knock on the door. I went over and glanced at the monitor. Eddie stood in the hallway. He was alone.

I twirled the locks and let him in. He nodded to me. "Heard you talking. Thought you might have company."

I nodded to the plant. "New plant."

"You're talking to your plants now?"

"They say it's good for them. Helps them grow." I shrugged. "I don't know if it's true or not. Couldn't hurt, right?"

Eddie remained standing. I pointed to the couch. "You want to sit down?"

"No, thanks. I can't stay. Just came by to tell you there's no word on Grover."

"You could've saved your breath. I already knew that."

"Vin and Roger have been pounding the pavement, asking around. Nobody's seen him."

"Maybe Butterface has gotten to him already."

"You really believe that?"

"No." A man like Grover wasn't about to be taken out by a man like Butterface. It wouldn't be right. That kind of cosmic injustice would have tilted the universe the wrong way.

Eddie looked at me. "Earlier today, when you wanted a drink …"

"Forget about it. Momentary weakness. I wasn't thinking straight."

"I'm not here to chide you, Jack. You're a big boy, you can look after yourself. You've come a long way, that's all."

"You don't want to see me backslide."

"No, I don't." Eddie smiled. "But it doesn't matter what I want. What matters is what you want."

"I want to find something on this guy Butterface before he kills me. He gave me forty-eight hours. Kill Grover, or Butterface kills me."

"He's mobbed up, Jack. Gotta be. How else would he know about Freddy and Tommy?"

"That's the problem with getting old in this game. Too many goddamn ghosts." I saw them at night sometimes. All the men I'd seen die over the years, their faces swimming out at me from the darkness. Sometimes their mouths were moving, like they had something to tell me. I could never quite make out what they were saying, but I imagined it was something like, *Come on, Jack. Join us. It's not so bad.*

Eddie turned to go. "Get some rest, Jack. Tomorrow is another day."

I closed the door behind him and twirled the locks. I sat down on the couch and stared across the room at my new plant. "Goodnight." It was hard to sleep while the Death Clock kept ticking. Forty-eight hours, and six of those hours were gone. It was 1:00 a.m., and it wasn't getting any earlier.

"Jack."

I blinked. I was lying down on the couch. The red digital numbers on my clock said 3:23. I must've dozed off. In my dreams the dead came visiting. The pale faces, the eyes lost in shadow, the lips moving with no sounds coming out. Then I heard the voice again. "Jack."

I sat up and there he was. Grover, with his trim little moustache and his all-white suit. He had pulled my desk chair out from behind the desk and wheeled it beside the couch. In his hand was a gun, and the gun was pointed right at me.

"What's the gag, Grover?"

"No gag." The gun didn't waver. "Heard you saw an acquaintance of mine earlier today."

"Richard?" I rubbed my eyes. "Technically that was yesterday."

Grover smirked. "Do you plan to die on a technicality?"

"I'm not planning to die at all. At least, not yet. Put that thing away, will you?"

Grover kept the gun levelled at me. "I heard a few more things, too. I heard Chester wants you to kill me, and then I heard you've got guys up and down the street beating the bushes looking for me. You gotta admit, Jack, that doesn't look good."

"Who the fuck is Chester?"

Grover frowned. "What did he say his name was?"

"He said to call him Richard."

"Richard, Chester. He's the same fucking guy. Who knows what the fuck his actual name is?"

"Seriously. Put that away. I was looking for you because I need more information."

"Oh yeah? About what?"

"About Richard. Chester. I've been calling him Mr.

Butterface. You know, because his face is all shiny. Why does he want you dead?"

"What you gotta understand, Jack, is that that guy is a moral void. He doesn't have wants or needs like you or me. He's a fucking lapdog. He does as he's told."

"So it's the mob."

"The mob. What's the mob? There's no 'mob,' Jack. There's just a bunch of guys who sit in a backroom and try to do business with each other."

"Those backroom boys want you dead."

"Well. That's something we have in common."

My cellphone rang. Grover gestured with his gun. "Go on. Answer it."

I flipped the phone open. "Yeah."

"Jack, it's Vin. I'm down here at Union Station. I talked to a guy who saw Grover hop on a train to New York. I don't think he's in the city anymore."

I looked over at Grover. "The guy who told you that? Don't give him any money."

"Jack?"

"Look, I gotta go. Knock off for the night, okay? We'll talk tomorrow."

I hung up. Grover and I sat in the darkness. I had a knife close by, but there was no way to get to it. One shot and it would be all over. Who would come to my funeral? Eddie, for sure. Maybe he'd get it catered. All those delicious little sandwiches.

"Who was it?"

"It was Vin. He said you'd hopped a train to New York."

Grover grinned. "New York in November?"

"Why not? There's worse times to go."

He stared at me. "You know, Jack, I've always envied your set-up here. You've got a lot of friends that care about you. I hope you know that."

"Are you one of those friends?"

He kept grinning. He didn't lower the gun. "Sure, Jack. I'm your friend."

"Then believe me. I'm not trying to kill you." I held up my hands. "Seems to me we've got the same problem. The same people want us dead, for the same reasons."

"Did you tell them I killed Freddy?"

"I didn't tell them shit."

Grover blinked. He lowered the gun. "I believe you." He sighed and ran his hands through his sandy-blond hair. "What did that prick tell you?"

"He said I have forty-eight hours to kill you, or he's going to kill me."

"Damn." Grover whistled, long and low. "That's a tight timeline."

"You're telling me."

He raised an eyebrow. "I don't think you're going to make it."

"No," I said. "I don't think I am."

Grover laughed. "Well, then. Let's talk about our options."

CHAPTER 22

The next morning, the sun didn't shine. It was another grey November day. The sky was like a smear of charcoal. Grover and I had breakfast in Eddie's restaurant. The place wasn't open for breakfast, but Eddie fried us some bacon and eggs anyway. Grover sliced his eggs daintily with his knife. I smashed into mine with the blunt side of my fork. The yolks bled yellow onto my plate.

We had talked all night. I sipped my coffee, feeling that jolt of caffeine to my system. Sooner or later I'd have to crash but not just yet.

Turned out Grover knew where Mr. Butterface hung his hat. The man rented a condo down on Queens Quay. After breakfast, that was our first stop. I went into the restaurant's kitchen and filled up a Thermos with coffee. I also grabbed an empty two-litre plastic bottle. Input, output. We were going to be sitting in Grover's car for awhile.

It was a straight shot down Spadina south to Queens Quay. Things got darker when we went under the

Gardiner. The big expressway blocked out what little sun there was. Then we came out the other side, and I could see the lake. The water looked as cold and grey as the sky. We kept driving.

Grover looked over at me and grinned. "Whose do you think is bigger?"

"Excuse me?"

"The prices on our heads. Whose do you think is bigger?"

"I've heard size doesn't matter."

"Oh really? You've heard that, huh?" Grover chuckled. "I think mine is probably bigger. I've caused way more damage than you."

"I guess it all depends on who Sammy hates more."

"You think this is DiAngelo, huh?"

"Either him or someone above him. Someone with enough juice to be a shot-caller."

Grover pointed. "That's the building right there." We pulled into a parking spot on the lake side of Queens Quay. A jogger went by, her feet slapping through the slush. I took a sip of coffee and settled back to wait.

"What do you know about DiAngelo?"

"I know he's a piece of shit. Does that count?"

"Is Butterface part of his crew?"

Grover nodded. "Butterface is freelance, but he's been working with them, yeah. He's the guy you see right before your lights go out."

"A killer for hire."

"More than that. Some hit men, you know, they can rationalize it. Like they're just soldiers following orders. Takes the moral calculus right out of the equation.

Butterface, though … he's a sadist. Probably a psychopath. The guy enjoys hurting people."

I thought back to Nadine refusing to answer my questions at the bar. "Yeah, I know."

"Anyway, that's who Sammy's sicced on us. If it was Sammy."

I looked over at Butterface's building. "With any luck, we'll know soon enough."

Even with the coffee, I was getting dozy. I wasn't a kid anymore. At eighteen, nineteen, I could catch fifteen minutes of sleep a night and still feel fresh as a daisy. Not so much anymore. I blinked and yawned. Grover looked over at me. "Go ahead and catch some Zs. I'll watch for Butterface."

It wasn't a bad idea. Problem was, just a few hours back Grover had pointed a gun right between my eyes. I didn't exactly feel comfortable enough to snuggle up in his car and go to sleep. "I'm fine." *C'mon, Butterface,* I thought. *Show your oily-looking self. Come on out of that building and go see your masters. Connect some dots for us.*

One thing Grover and I had going for us was that we weren't policemen. The burden of proof we were looking for didn't have to stand up in any court of law. We just had to tie Butterface to DiAngelo by any means necessary.

And then what? Grover would want to kill them both. I wasn't exactly against the idea. I was sure the world would be a better place without Butterface skipping merrily through fields of daisies, a big smile on his face and his hands dripping blood. And DiAngelo had been making my life a living hell for a while now.

But maybe, just maybe, Butterface wasn't working with DiAngelo. Maybe there was a new shot-caller on the horizon. Someone unknown to Grover or myself, some shadowy someone who wanted the both of us dead and buried. That was what we were here to find out.

I shifted in the leather seat. Barely an hour and my legs were already going numb. I sipped more coffee. It was bitter, almost sour.

Grover straightened up. "There he is."

"Where?"

"Right the fuck there. Coming out of the building."

I followed Grover's finger. He was right. Mr. Butterface stood on the sidewalk wearing that same long grey trench coat he had been wearing when he braced me by the Dufferin Gate. He wasn't wearing his fedora, though. His head was vaguely pumpkin shaped. A few strands of dirty-blond hair fluttered in the breeze blowing cold off the lake.

Grover reached down, twisted the keys, and fired up the engine. "The bastard's hailing a cab. Keep watching him, Jack."

"I see him. He's headed westbound."

Grover slammed the car into gear and pulled a U-turn. Car horns blared. "Yeah, yeah," he muttered. We were three cars behind Butterface's cab. Grover looked over at me and winked. "We're on him now."

Hopefully the man wasn't going someplace boring, like the grocery store or the barber. I didn't feel like shadowing Butterface as he did his daily chores.

I shouldn't have worried. The cab headed north on Spadina. We followed, heading back under the

Gardiner. The cab continued north through Chinatown. I squirmed in my seat. This was too close for comfort. I breathed a sigh of relief when Butterface's cab passed Eddie's building without even slowing down.

The cab turned west on College. We were only two cars back now. I was starting to worry that Butterface would spot us and lead us on a wild goose chase. *You like driving, boys? Let me take you on a tour of Toronto's scenic warehouse parking lots.* The cab continued west past Bathurst and on into Little Italy.

I turned to Grover. "Slow down."

"What?"

"Slow down! He's stopping."

Butterface's cab pulled up to the curb and stopped. We slid into a parking spot and kept the engine running, just in case. Butterface got out and went into a joint called the Café Veronica. Grover reached for the keys to turn off the engine, but I shook my head. "Cab's still there."

"Maybe he's waiting for another fare."

"Yeah, maybe. Or maybe he's waiting for Butterface."

After about five minutes, Butterface strolled out of the café. He was carrying a brown leather briefcase. Grover and I shot each other looks. "How's your bankroll these days, Jack?"

"You know how it is. This economy …"

Grover grunted. "The economy's fine. You're just lazy."

"I'm lazy?"

He flashed his teeth like a shark. "There's opportunity everywhere. Streets are paved with gold, my boy!"

"So what are you saying? You want to jack Butterface for his case?"

"I guarantee you there's money in there. I guaran-fucking-tee it."

Butterface got back into the cab and it pulled away. Grover waited until it was almost out of sight and then pulled out into traffic. Once again, horns blared. He looked up into the rear-view and shot the horn-blower the finger. Then he turned to me and smiled. "I tell ya, Jack. This city. It's like everyone's forgotten how to drive."

You're the one who cut him off, I thought but didn't say. We followed the cab all the way west until College Street turned into Dundas Street West. Then we went north to Roncesvalles. I wasn't too crazy about this part of the city. I always got turned around. Streets twisted and turned and fed into each other, and all the streets had the same name. Indian Grove Crescent, Indian Grove Circle, Indian Grove Lane. How could I be on the corner of Indian Grove and Indian Grove? Luckily for me, the cab didn't disappear into the warren of residential streets. It stopped outside an apartment building right on Roncesvalles. Grover sailed past the cab and parked a few spots north. Butterface climbed out of the cab and carried his briefcase into the apartment building. Once again, the cab waited for him. When he came out of the building, he was no longer carrying the case.

Grover was staring at the apartment building. "Now that's interesting."

"What is?"

"We'll have to come back here. I've got a hunch." He twisted the wheel and once again we were following the cab. I was starting to get nervous. Any second now Butterface could look up and catch a glimpse of us in the cab's rear-view. It turned out he wasn't looking for tails, though. The man was feeling confident. With any luck, that confidence would be his downfall.

CHAPTER 23

The rest of Butterface's morning was uneventful. Grover and I sat and waited while he got a haircut at a barbershop back in Little Italy. I was half hoping someone else would walk into the shop and blow him away on the barber chair, but it didn't happen. Butterface got a trim and then a hot shave with the towels and the lather and the straight razor and everything. He walked out grinning like a million bucks.

He took the cab back to his condo. Grover and I sat in the car across the street. Far out on the lake was a boat heading for distant shores. Grover looked over at me. "What do you think? Do we stay on him?"

"Nah. That's enough for the day."

"I'll drop you off at Eddie's. Hey, Jack?"

"Yeah?"

"This was fun. We should hang out more often, you and me."

The woman in the silver sequined top was back at Eddie's casino, only this morning she wasn't wearing her sequins. She was wearing a white button-up blouse and she had her hair pulled back in a ponytail. From the looks of her chip stack, she was doing well. Once again I thought of my ex Cassandra. Wherever she was, I hoped her chip stack was growing, too.

Eddie was lounging back on a barstool, taking in the action. I sauntered over and sat down next to him.

"How's tricks, Eddie?"

"Been a good morning. Shitty weather like this, people don't want to go outside. They want to stay in here where it's nice and warm and lose all their money."

I tilted my chin at the woman in the white shirt. "She seems to be doing well."

"Uh-uh, Jack. Don't you do it."

"Do what?"

"Do what, he says. Don't you fall for another poker player."

"She's doing well, that's all. I'm not falling for anyone." That last sentence wasn't exactly true. Suzanne was back in town, and it was her face I was seeing when I closed my eyes. "I'm going to go crash for a bit. Do you know anything about Café Veronica?"

Eddie tapped his chin. "That joint in Little Italy?"

"Yeah. I think I saw a bag man coming out of there this morning."

"I'll ask around."

"Thanks, Eddie."

I walked up to my office and rattled the windows. How the fuck did Grover keep getting in here? *Maybe*

I should get a hotel room, I thought. Someplace nice, without cigarette burns on the comforter.

For now, the couch would have to do. I lay down with the neon lights of Chinatown blaring through my window. There was a feeble trickle of sunlight, too, as the sun tried to break through the November grey. I closed my eyes and thought of Suzanne. Suzanne, Suzanne, Suzanne. Almost a decade later, and there was still something there. Then again, that was what I had thought about Cassandra, too. Turned out these days, Cassandra was batting for the other team. That was to say, she liked women and always had. Suzanne, though ... she liked men, and I thought she still liked me. It had been a while since I had thought of that fantasy cabin in the woods, but it still sounded appealing. Just packing up and bugging out, away from all the strife and striving of the world.

I suddenly sat bolt upright. The solution to my money woes had been staring me in the face all along. It meant shuttering Palace Security, at least for now, but I could live with that. Fuck it, I'd tried.

I took the stairs two at a time, heading down to the casino. The woman in the white shirt was still there and she was still winning. I wondered if she was a shill, a hired player brought in by Eddie to keep things interesting. If she was, she'd split her winnings with Eddie at the end of the night. But Eddie had always run a more or less clean house, which meant the woman's winnings were probably legit.

"Eddie!" The big man looked up. It was morning but he hadn't slept yet, so I supposed it was okay that he had a glass of Scotch in his hand. "Remember The Chief's lawyer?"

Eddie wrinkled his brow. "Oh, yeah. That sunburnt guy who looked like he was running coke all over the Florida Keys."

"That's the guy. Do you remember his name?"

"Rhodes, wasn't it? Calvin Rhodes. No, wait — Kevin."

I snapped my fingers. "That's it! Do you still have his business card kicking around?"

I followed Eddie to his office and waited while he rummaged through his desk drawers. He pulled out a fistful of lollipops and a loaded .45. The gun thunked on the desk as he set it down. "Ah, there it is."

He passed me the card. I smiled and slapped him on the shoulder. "Thanks, Eddie."

"You need some lawyering? Because I've got a guy better than Rhodes."

"No, Rhodes is good. Mind if I use your phone?"

Rhodes's phone rang once, twice, three times. A woman's voice answered. "Rhodes and Associates."

"Is Kevin in?"

"One moment, please."

The hold music was crackly and full of static. I never understood that. In this day and age, why was hold music so crappy? With today's technology, the music should be coming in with crystal clarity. We could put a man on the moon, but —

"Kevin Rhodes. How may I help you?"

"Mr. Rhodes, this is Jack Palace. A few months back you gave me the deed to The Chief's trailer."

"Yeah, I remember. What can I do for you, Jack?"

The Chief's trailer was gone, but the land remained. Twenty-five acres of prime Southern Ontario real estate. I took a deep breath before I continued. "I want to sell the place."

CHAPTER 24

I t felt right. At first I thought it might feel like a be-
trayal, like somehow I was letting The Chief down.
But it didn't feel like that at all. I could almost feel The
Chief grinning down at me from wherever he was. He
had helped me plenty in life, and now, in death, he was
helping me again. The land might take a while to sell,
but when it did, I would have a sack of cash, free and
clear. Enough to move away. Enough to start again. I
went back up to my office and drifted off with a big
smile on my face.

When I woke up, I couldn't breathe. I choked and
lashed out with my arms and legs. There was nobody there.
I caught my breath and lay there panting on the couch.

Goddamn dreams. Whoever or whatever I'd been
fighting while I slept receded as consciousness returned.
I glanced over at the clock: 2:00 p.m. I thought about
Butterface and his forty-eight-hour countdown. He was
going to be damn disappointed that I wouldn't make it.

Or maybe he'd be happy, who knows? If the forty-eight-hour timeline was legit, me blowing the deadline would mean that Butterface would be let off the leash to kill me dead. That was where the term "deadline" had originated. It was an actual line drawn or carved in the dirt around a prison. If the prisoners stepped over that line, *pow*. They were shot dead.

I had the wheels in motion to buy my fabled cabin in the woods, and now I had to buy myself some more time. In order to do that, I had to meet up with Butterface. I wasn't sure what I was going to tell him, exactly, but I figured I would think of something when the time came.

I went down to Eddie's restaurant with my stomach rumbling. Two o'clock was late for lunch. At least, it was late for me. There were still plenty of people in the restaurant. The smell of sizzling beef and soy sauce filled the air. I ordered shrimp, spare ribs, and dumplings. Everything was hot and fresh. I tucked in with gusto.

It was nice to feel full. I didn't stuff myself — no need to be a glutton — but I ate just the right amount. I looked up and saw a man on the other side of the plate glass window quickly look away. He hustled away. I watched him go. It wasn't Butterface. It was another man in a suit. He had a short, sharp face like a weasel. I got the feeling he had been watching me.

Had he been sent by Butterface? While Grover and I had been watching Butterface, had Butterface's goons been watching us? Wheels within wheels. Man, I hated this shit. I was itching for a straight-up fight. One punch, guy goes down, end of story. All this cloak-and-dagger shit was making me dizzy.

After lunch I walked through the Chinatown crowds to the bar. Just a beer, just one, maybe two. I couldn't do it. I found a seat with my back to the wall, and I drank my club soda slow.

"Jack." Grover, grinning, pulled up a chair and sat down beside me. His back was to the wall, too. It must've looked odd, two grown men sitting side by side in a bar that had plenty of open seats.

I frowned. "You gotta fade into the shadows. We're being watched."

"Fuck 'em, let 'em watch." The server came over and Grover ordered a beer. He drank it in three long gulps. "You know, I've been thinking. This whole forty-eight-hours thing is bullshit. You think Butterface is biding his time watching a clock? I say fuck that. He's going to come after you and me both." Grover's lips pulled back to reveal his teeth. He reminded me of a wolverine. "I say we hit him first and we hit him hard. Let him know who he's fucking with."

I tilted my head. "That doesn't sound like you."

Grover frowned. "It's me talking, isn't it? Who else would I sound like?"

"There was a man watching me while I ate lunch today."

"Butterface?"

"No. He looked like a weasel in a suit. Maybe a ferret. You know, something in the weasel family."

Grover kept frowning. "I don't know what you're talking about."

"What he looked like didn't matter. Someone's keeping tabs on us. They're probably watching us right now.

And if you're sitting there hatching plans, they're going to cotton on to those plans, too."

Grover leaned toward me. "The only way they're going to figure out my plans is if you tell them." He leaned back. "I say fuck 'em. If they're gunning for us, we're gunning for them." He grinned. "Just like the good old days, right, Jack?"

Not exactly. "I can't just walk up to Butterface and kill him."

"No, you can't." Grover stood up. "But I can."

I followed Grover out onto the sidewalk but the little man was already gone. How did he do that? Being little helped, no doubt. He could fade into the crowds easier than I ever could.

I turned and Ferret Face was standing there watching me. My eyes went to his hands. *Always watch the hands*, The Chief had told me many moons ago. *They can't pull anything on you if you always watch the hands.*

"Come on," Ferret Face said, "the boss wants to see you."

"Fuck off," I replied. "I'm busy."

Ferret Face flinched like I had slapped him upside the head. "I'm trying to make your life easier here. There's no need to be rude."

"Who are you working for?"

"Let's talk in the car."

I took a step forward. "I don't think so." My hand flickered toward the knife beneath my coat.

Ferret Face took a step back. "Easy, now. I'm unarmed."

"Tell me who you're working for. Is it Richard?"

"Who?"

"Chester? Whatever his name is."

Ferret Face shook his head. "I don't know what you're talking about. I work for Mr. Rhodes."

I blinked. "The lawyer?"

"Yeah, that's right. Your lawyer. Come on, he needs you to sign some papers."

Turned out Ferret Face was legit. He was a legman for Kevin Rhodes, Attorney at Law. Ferret Face's real name was Ben Tupperman. Ben drove me to Kevin Rhodes's office, and I signed some paperwork authorizing Rhodes to sell The Chief's property on my behalf. I signed and pushed the papers across his desk. Rhodes shuffled the pages together and stared at me. "Say, while you're here … do you have a will?"

"Are you threatening me?"

Rhodes chuckled and held up his hands. "Easy, now. I'm just asking. Say this sale goes through, but something happens to you. Where do you want the money to go?"

"Suzanne." I blinked, realizing the rightness of the words.

"Last name?"

I told him. "Leave everything to her."

"I'll prepare the document." It took Rhodes about forty minutes to get it together. The damn thing was seven pages long and full of legalese. He charged me six hundred bucks. Seemed like a long and expensive way of saying "Suzanne gets everything," but that was the game, and I had to play it.

"Now then, Jack," Rhodes said, smiling like the cat who caught the canary, "is there anything else I can help you with?"

I stood up. "Just sell the damn place."

Out on the sidewalk a cold wind was blowing. I hopped on the subway and headed back toward Chinatown. At Spadina station I transferred to the streetcar. There was a woman sitting opposite me — a girl, really, probably in her early twenties. She had short hair dyed a purplish red, and her eyes were covered in sparkly face paint. Her headphones were on and she was grooving to the tunes. I wondered what she was listening to. I doubted it was anything I had ever heard of, but she sure seemed to be enjoying it. For a brief moment, our eyes locked. I shot her what I hoped was a reassuring, nonthreatening smile. She smiled back. I looked away and she went right on grooving.

Suzanne was waiting for me inside Eddie's casino. She had a rum and Coke in front of her. Since when did she like rum? She tilted her chin at the poker player in the white blouse. "She's good."

I nodded. "She's very good."

"You got a minute?"

I thought of Butterface and the ticking clock. "Yeah, sure."

"I want to ask you something, and I want an honest

answer. Okay?" I didn't say anything. I could feel my heart speed up in my chest. "Okay?"

"Yeah, sure. Shoot."

"If you and I got back together, what would it be like?"

I smiled. "Only one way to find out."

"I'm serious, Jack. Let's cut the bullshit. I like you, you like me. Life is precious, and life is short." She stared right into my eyes. "I don't want to waste any time. I want to know right now. Are you with me in this or not?"

I took her hand. "I'm with you."

She didn't say anything. Then, she smiled. "Just like that."

"Yeah. Just like that."

She pulled her hand away. "But it's not that easy, is it? You have your work. The price on your head. You still need to get all that straight."

"That's right. I do and I will."

"And in the meantime ..."

"In the meantime, it's probably best if you don't come around. Hunker down somewhere safe —"

"Oh, balls."

"What?"

"Nowhere's safe. Isn't that right? If they come for you, they come for you."

I shook my head. "They're coming for me, not you." I reached for her hand again. She let me take it. "I've got some land up north. No, wait, listen to me. I'm not saying go up there and hide. I'm selling the land. We're going to use the money to buy that cabin. Do you understand? Everything we want. It's close. It's so damn close I can taste it."

She looked at me and smiled with her full ruby lips. Her eyes were half-lidded. "Well?"

"Well, what?"

"What are you waiting for?"

I leaned in, and we kissed.

You know that old cliché about fireworks? Sometimes, that shit is true. I kissed Suzanne and it was like a whole freakin' fireworks factory was exploding in my head.

We stumbled up the stairs together, tugging at our clothes. I unlocked all the locks while Suzanne fumbled with my belt. We pushed inside my office, slamming against a stack of boxes and knocking two of them to the ground. We made it over to the couch without knocking over anything else.

I got her shirt off, she got my pants off, and we went from there. I undid her pants and slipped my hand inside. She gasped a short little gasp as my fingers dipped into her folds. I yanked her pants off and then I pushed aside her black-lace panties, revealing those luscious lips. I pushed her down on the couch and thrust inside. She was hot and wet and ready. "Jack …" she moaned. "Jack …"

We tumbled and twisted on the couch. She straddled me, riding hard, then I grabbed her and flipped her over onto her hands and knees. I clasped her hips and pushed inside, hard, trying to jam as much of myself inside her as I could. She was gasping, breasts bobbing as we rocked back and forth together.

Another fireworks factory exploded when I came. I shuddered, pumping deep inside her body.

She rubbed up against me. "Put your fingers inside me, Jack." I slid two fingers inside her slick folds. She rubbed herself as I moved my fingers in and out. She moaned and then gasped and arched her back.

We lay there together, our sweat mingling, me lying on the couch and Suzanne lying on top of me. She pushed back her hair and smiled. "In the movies, this is when I'd be lighting up a cigarette."

"You don't smoke."

"Nope." She traced a finger through my chest hair and then looked around my office. "What's up with all these boxes?"

"They're Eddie's. He's been using the office as a storage room."

"So you don't live here?"

"I guess I do for now."

She kept smiling. "Until that cabin money comes in."

"Yeah, that's right." I could feel her heartbeat. Maybe she could feel mine, too. "It's going to happen, babe."

She looked at me and nodded slowly. "Yeah. Maybe it will."

CHAPTER 25

Grover had gone to ground. I couldn't raise him on any of the regular channels. Eddie wasn't having any luck, either. I figured Grover was busy out there, stalking his prey. For the first time, I wondered whether Butterface's offer was legit. Kill Grover and skate off into the sunset. Of course, I couldn't kill Grover, but the thought of putting my problems behind me was a good one.

The sun was going down, swallowed up by the black clouds. I missed the golden summer sunsets. There'd be time for that. Suzanne and I could sit on the cabin's porch and watch the sun disappear behind the trees. It was going to happen.

Yeah, sure, Jack. Just like Palace Security, right?

Palace Security had happened. It just hadn't lasted long. Nothing in life lasts. That's why we have to hold on to the sweet moments for as long as we can.

Suzanne had gone back to the apartment she was renting in Kensington Market. It was a few streets away from her old place. She was on a real nostalgia trip, I thought. Going back to the old and familiar after her world was rocked by her man Steve dying. Brain cancer, man. What a horrible way to go. *Beats being tortured to death by mobsters, though, doesn't it, Jack?* I was part of Suzanne's nostalgia trip, but it didn't bother me any. She and I weren't looking back, we were looking ahead. Sure, we were dreaming, but that's how everything starts: with a dream. Everything around us — cars, radios, televisions, every invention right down to the homes we live in and the clothes we wear — was once a figment of someone else's dream.

It was time to dream my dream. I'd thought it was Palace Security, but it wasn't. The real dream was the same one it had always been: retirement. Walking away from the old life. Suzanne had said I'd always be a fighter, and I knew she was right. I'd always need to fight someone or something, at least until I was old and grey. And then, who knows? I was more mellow today than I had been as an angry nineteen-year-old, burning with rage. In ten more years, twenty … who knows?

Assuming, of course, that I made it that far.

I went down to Eddie's casino. The woman poker player wasn't there. Even the best of us have to sleep sometimes. Eddie was perched on his usual barstool, his back to the bar, scoping out the action. He saw me coming and smiled. "Suzanne, huh?"

"Don't start."

"I'm not starting anything. I'm happy for you, that's all." He kept smiling. "I'm happy for you both." He snapped his fingers. "That reminds me. That police report you asked for? My guy came through."

He stood up and together we walked into his office. Eddie picked up a manila envelope from his desk and passed it over to me. I opened it up. There was Butterface, staring up at me from a police mug shot. Eddie pointed his lollipop at the pic. "I took a gander at his file. This guy's a real piece of work, Jack. Killer for hire. Likes to hurt women. If you ask me, he's a stone-cold psychopath."

I flipped through the file. Butterface's real name was Lester Richards. Lester, Chester. Richards, Richard. His aliases made sense. He had been arrested nine times, starting with an assault case when he was just eighteen. He'd beaten a girl bloody and left her for dead in a dumpster. My hands curled into fists. I uncurled my fists and pushed the file away. "Grover's planning to take this guy off the board."

Eddie nodded. "I don't think anyone will weep too much. Oh, and that café in Little Italy you were asking about? You were right. It's one of DiAngelo's. Not directly, but the man who owns it kicks up to DiAngelo."

"So Butterface is connected to DiAngelo."

"So what? DiAngelo's already got a hit out on you. What's he going to do, kill you twice?"

I stared at Eddie. "Is that supposed to be reassuring?"

"I'm just saying, is all. This guy Butterface is a piece of shit. The world will be better off without him."

"No argument here." I stared down at the file. "It's just …"

"Oh, no. Don't you start."

"Start what?"

"I know you, Jack. You're trying to think of a way out of this DiAngelo situation and you're thinking you can reason with these guys. Grover's methods may be blunt, but in this case, he's got the right idea."

"So Grover kills Butterface. As you say, no great loss. But then Sammy DiAngelo and his crew send someone else. And then someone after him. And then someone after him. They're not going to stop until I'm dead." I leaned back. "There's only one solution I can see. I've got to convince DiAngelo that I'm worth more to him alive."

"How the hell are you going to do that?"

I smiled. "That, my friend, is a damn good question."

Grover came to me again that night. I was up on the rooftop, a.k.a. the asphalt beach. I was freezing my butt off, but I couldn't sleep, and I needed some fresh air. Grover walked up to me like he was strolling down a country lane. "I heard you were looking for me."

"Grover, how the fuck did you get up here?"

His teeth flashed in the darkness. "Uh uh, Jack. A magician never reveals his secrets."

"Hold off on the Butterface hit."

Grover scowled. "You drinking again?"

"I'm serious. He's connected with DiAngelo, and I don't know how tight. Lay off until I figure that out."

"You're already in a pit with DiAngelo. Digging yourself in deeper isn't going to do any harm."

"It's going to make it harder to climb out, that's all." I leaned forward. Grover smelled like sandalwood and leather. "I'm not saying don't do it. I'm just asking you to wait."

Grover shrugged. "Since you put it that way …" He laughed. "Of all the guys in the world to go to bat for, you go to bat for fucking Chester."

"His real name is Lester."

"Oh really? You know I don't give a shit, right?"

The wind whipped at my coat and slapped my face. Grover stepped closer. "Your forty-eight hours is up tomorrow, Jack. Don't you think it would be better if Butterface wasn't around by then?"

I had to admit, the man had a point. Butterface had given me forty-eight hours to either kill Grover or be killed myself. Kill or be killed. I didn't like either option. Maybe it was time to send a message to DiAngelo that I didn't like being pushed around. "Killing Butterface would be self-defence, right?"

"That's one way of looking at it."

"You know what? Do it."

Grover grinned. "Consider it done. Oh, one more thing. I've been watching that apartment house on Roncesvalles. The one where Butterface dropped off the briefcase. I think I've got it figured out. It's a counting house, Jack. DiAngelo money from all over the city flows to the counting house. Bags get dropped off in one apartment, someone else comes in and brings the bags upstairs to the counting room. I took a little peek inside. They've got counting machines going 24-7. There's a safe in there, too. We're talking big fucking money." Grover kept grinning. "You've been wanting to retire, right?"

"You're saying we rob Sammy DiAngelo's counting house?"

The wind howled. Grover tapped his temple. "Right on the money."

I stared at the little man. "You want to come inside, get a drink?"

He stared out at the city lights. "You go ahead. I'm going to stay up here and watch the city awhile."

CHAPTER 26

Robbing Sammy DiAngelo's counting house. It seemed like suicide. I wasn't scared of Sammy, but the logistics didn't look good. How to get in, how to get out?

It also meant going to war. Grover was right when he said I was already in a pit with Sammy. I didn't want to go to war, but the war had found me. My last shot at a peaceful resolution had died with Freddy, back when Grover slit his throat. Or maybe a peaceful resolution had always been a pipe dream. Maybe it was always going to come down to either me on top or Sammy DiAngelo standing over me with his boot on my neck.

I sat in my office surrounded by boxes. The couch still smelled like Suzanne: the smell of warm vanilla cookies. I glanced over at the plant on my desk. "Whaddaya say, Plant? Is it war?"

Mr. Plant, he didn't say nothin'.

At some point I must've drifted off to sleep because when I woke up, the pale light of dawn was sneaking through my window. I knew I had to make one last-ditch effort to talk to Sammy DiAngelo and resolve things. The problem was, I no longer had any go-betweens. I couldn't go back to Freddy's old joint on the Danforth, not after the fight with Bobby the Beast and his buddy. There was one guy I could try, an old man who had retired from the game. Mario had worked for The Old Man back when The Old Man was running the rackets. I didn't want to drag Mario into anything, but I figured it couldn't hurt to talk.

Eddie was asleep behind his desk when I stepped into his office. The big man blinked and rubbed his eyes. "What time is it?"

"It's morning. Listen, I need to borrow a car."

"You got it." Eddie sat up straight. He yawned. "You want me to send Vin along for the ride?"

"No, it's nothing like that. I just have to go out to Hamilton to see an old friend."

"You sure? Vin's not doing anything this morning. I got Roger and another guy watching the casino. You know Vin, he could be helpful."

"Thanks, but no thanks. This is a solo trip."

Eddie shrugged. "All right, man. Suit yourself."

Vin pulled the Camry up to the back door of Eddie's building. He climbed out and kept the motor running. "You sure you don't want me to come with?"

"Nah. This is just a friendly little visit, that's all."

"All right, Jack. Safe driving."

I took the 403 south. Traffic was bad but mostly going the other way. Commuters piling into the city to start another day of work. Mario lived up on the mountain, and that was where I was headed. The old man lived a quiet life now with his wife, tending his grapevines and his apricot trees. He was proof that it could be done.

From the outside, his house was neat and tidy and well cared for, and the inside was no different. I kicked off my shoes in the front hall, and Mario ushered me into the living room. A large crucified Jesus hung on the wall, a mournful look on his face, like he was saying, *Why me?*

I had called ahead. Mario's wife was ready with a massive platter of cookies and a pitcher of fizzy punch. If it had been later in the day, the punch would've been wine. I took two cookies to be polite and then I took a third because they were good. Mario leaned back on the couch. I sat opposite him in an overstuffed armchair. "Thanks for seeing me, Mario."

The old man smiled. "What else am I going to do? I'm here, you know, I water the plants, I feed the birds. It's nice to see you, my friend."

We bantered for a bit. Grandkids? Doing well. Little Johnny was on the soccer team. Me and Suzanne? Yes, that seemed like it was going places. It was good to have someone in your life. We agreed on that. Mrs. Mario (I never did know her actual name) came in and refilled the drinks. Then she hustled away, back to the back of the house.

"Mario," I said finally, "I need your help."

"What can I do? You come to see me, I know it's not a social call."

"There's a man who doesn't like me."

Mario chuckled. "That's life, right? Not everybody can like everybody."

"True enough. But this guy, he really, really doesn't like me."

"And you need my help for lessons on how to be charming. How to — what was that book? *How to Win Friends and Influence People*."

"Yeah, something like that. I need help setting up a meeting. I want to sit down and talk to this guy, see if we can work something out."

Mario nodded. "It's good to work things out. This man who doesn't like you — what's the name?"

"Sammy DiAngelo."

"Sammy." Mario made a whooshing sound. He sipped his fizzy drink. "Sure, I remember Sammy. Maybe he's changed over the years, but when I knew him, he was a hothead. A volcano of a man."

"He's moved up in the world."

"So I hear, so I hear. Maybe I can do this thing for you. Set up a meeting someplace nice and safe for everyone. I can set it up, Jack, but I can't make him listen."

"Understood. You can lead a horse to water, but you can't make him drink."

"Yes, yes, that's it exactly. You're a smart man, Jack."

Would a smart man be trying to meet with Sammy DiAngelo? I wasn't too sure, but I had to try.

I stood up and shook Mario's hand. "Thank you, Mario. I owe you one."

The old man smiled. "Maybe you do. Maybe you can repay the favour someday."

I got back in my car and drove home, Mario's parting line still ringing in my ears. That bit about repaying the favour seemed a little ominous to me, but maybe my mind was just in a dark place. Maybe it was just banter. Either way, I had gotten what I came for, so I had to be happy. I was going to meet the "king."

Sammy DiAngelo was a king only in his own mind. The Old Man's rackets had diminished quite a bit over the past ten years. People had gotten killed, people had gotten locked up, and people had gone their separate ways. There were at least four crews with their roots in The Old Man's operations, and Sammy's crew was just one of the four. Sammy had only about fifteen guys under him, but just one with a gun was enough to kill me dead.

Maybe something would come of the meeting, maybe not. If I walked out alive, I'd consider it a success. In the meantime, I wanted to see Suzanne again. I wanted her to get out of town. I had a feeling things were about to get messy.

I knew she wouldn't go easy. She was starting to rebuild her life after the life she'd built in Saskatoon had collapsed like a house of cards. It wasn't her fault. People got sick every day. Things could change just like that. I felt bad for Steve, her man who'd died of brain cancer, a man I had never met. Hopefully he and Suzanne had packed in a lot of living while he was alive. Hopefully Suzanne and I would pack a lot into our lives, too.

I pulled the Camry into the alley behind Eddie's building and cut the engine. Then I flipped out my phone and punched in Suzanne's number.

"Hello?"

"Suzanne, it's me."

"Is everything okay?"

"Not much has changed. Put it that way. But I'm working on it."

She laughed. "Fair enough." She paused. "I had fun last night."

"Me, too. Are you around for lunch?"

"Can't do it today. I have a job interview. Some new tourist joint down on King West, over by the theatres."

"You might want to skip that."

There was a pause on the other end. "What do you mean?"

"Just hear me out. I know how you feel about this, but … things are getting a little dicey. I really think it would be best if you got out of town for a while."

Silence.

"Suzanne? You there?"

"This shit again."

"I just want you to be safe, that's all."

"I am safe, Jack."

"Maybe, but you'd be safer somewhere else."

"Where am I going to go? Huh?"

"You must still have friends in Saskatoon."

"I do. But Saskatoon is a long way away."

"That's sort of the whole point. Look, I'm going to wrap this up. I promise."

"When, Jack? When do we get to that pot of gold at the end of the rainbow?"

"Soon. And then —"

"I know. And then it's you and me and peaches and cream forever and ever, amen."

The line went dead. "Hello? Suzanne? Hello?"

Shit. That hadn't gone well.

I took a deep breath and stepped out of the Camry. The cold stung my hands. I needed to buy a pair of gloves.

I walked into Eddie's restaurant with the car keys jingling in my hand. And then I froze. Sitting at a table near the back of the restaurant was Butterface.

He saw me walk in and smiled. "Mr. Palace. May I call you Jack?" He held up his hands. "Don't worry, the clock is still ticking. You have until seven tonight. I just thought I'd stop by and try the lunch special. "

I stepped closer. My hands involuntarily turned into fists at my sides. "You need to stand up, walk out that door, and never come back."

The hit man remained sitting. "Where's your sense of hospitality?" He expertly used his chopsticks to lift another piece of pork to his mouth, sat there chewing, then swallowed. "Seven o'clock tonight, Jack. Then things either get easier for you, or a whole lot messier." He stood up, peeled a few bills from a wad of money, and dropped them onto the table. "Try the pork, it's not bad. Be seeing you."

Butterface turned his back to me. I contemplated stabbing him right in the back of the neck. Deep enough to sever his spinal cord and I could watch him fall like a marionette with its strings clipped. But then Eddie's restaurant would have to close down for the police investigation, and the casino would have to shut down, too. Plus stabbing someone in the neck in front of dozens of witnesses didn't seem like the smartest idea.

Butterface walked out, and I followed him. He glanced back to see me following and stopped on the sidewalk right in front of Eddie's restaurant. His breath escaped his slash of a mouth in huge steamy puffs. "Do the right thing here, Jack. You do this thing for us and your world gets a little brighter."

I kept calm. *Breathe in, breathe out.* "Fuck you."

Butterface raised his hand and hailed a passing cab. "It's too bad we had to meet this way." He reached out and opened the cab's back door. "In another world, we could've been friends."

"You're a psycho who likes to hurt women. I would never be friends with a piece of shit like you."

The man stiffened, then his easy smile returned. "The choice is yours, Mr. Palace. I'll see you around."

The cab sped off. If I hustled, maybe I could get to the Camry and follow. And then what? Time was getting tight. Seven o'clock was only seven hours away.

Even if Grover managed to kill Butterface between now and then, Butterface was only the messenger. My meeting with DiAngelo was set for five o'clock this evening in Little Italy, at the Café Veronica. Mario had come through.

I went down to the casino and slapped the keys to the Camry into Eddie's waiting palm. "I almost killed a man in your restaurant just now."

Eddie's eyebrows shot up. "Thanks for exercising some restraint."

"Hey, you owe me one." I smiled and he smiled back. "I'm meeting DiAngelo tonight. I'll need some backup."

"Vin and Roger."

"Maybe not Roger. That guy's got a bad attitude."

"You know what they say. It's hard to find good help these days."

"I'm going out there now to scope it out."

"You going to talk to Grover?"

"What do you mean?"

Eddie shrugged. "I'm just saying. You get Grover up on a nearby rooftop with a high-powered rifle, and all of this could be over real quick."

"Grover's got his own shit going on."

"Well, I might know a guy."

I shook my head. "No guns."

"That's you all over. Always bringing a knife to a gunfight."

"This is just a friendly little chat between me and DiAngelo. Hopefully we clear the air."

"This guy's got a price on your head, Jack. You're walking into a trap."

"I don't think so. Mario brokered this meeting. We've got a temporary truce. DiAngelo will honour that."

"You think so? Seems to me you're putting your eggs into a very dangerous basket."

"A basket full of snakes?"

"Yeah, exactly."

"I've got to try, Eddie." I knew it was a long shot, but I had to try. If DiAngelo would somehow agree to a long-term truce, then Suzanne and I could jet off into the sunset. Sayonara, City. Hello, Cabin in the Country.

Little Italy was bustling. I stepped through the crowds and went down the alley behind Café Veronica. It was just an alley, like hundreds of others. Garbage cans, brick walls, loops and swirls of graffiti. A cook in white was taking a smoke break out behind the restaurant. I nodded to him and kept going.

If I had to, I could escape through the kitchen and into the alley. Or so I told myself. If DiAngelo decided to betray Mario and break the truce, they'd be shipping me out of the café in a body bag.

I went to a nearby bar. I didn't even think about it. My legs carried me inside and parked me at a table facing the wall. A beautiful dark-haired server came by. Her eyes were violet. "Scotch," I told her. "No, wait. Club soda."

"You need a few more minutes?"

"I need a few more days."

"Sir?"

"Just the club soda." The server walked away. I sat listening to the bar patrons' clatter and buzz. The server returned with my club soda. As I drank it I looked around the room at all the regular folks who weren't meeting with a mobster later tonight. Of course, what did I know? Maybe there were all kinds of people in here meeting mobsters later. Maybe I wasn't that goddamn special after all.

I finished my drink and left the server a big tip. Then I walked out of there and caught the College streetcar back toward Chinatown.

CHAPTER 27

Vin volunteered to walk with me into the lion's den. I had spent the last few hours down in the casino, biding my time and remembering to breathe. The woman in the white shirt had returned, only this time she was wearing a black shirt. This time I smiled at her, and she smiled back. There, now we were old friends.

I turned to Vin and nodded. "You ready?"

"Ready. Let's go."

We took the Camry. Wouldn't be right to take the streetcar to a meeting like this. What if it broke down and we were late? Of course, traffic was traffic no matter what you were riding in, so we left plenty early. Vin glided the car west on College toward the Café Veronica. I wasn't entirely sure what I wanted to say to DiAngelo, but I knew the gist. It went something like this: stop being a fucking idiot and trying to have me killed. But, you know, more sugary than that. You can catch more flies with honey and all that jive.

Vin pulled up in front of the café, just like in the movies. You know how there's always a spot right out front? No one wants to waste screen time watching the hero try to parallel park and then walk three blocks.

We climbed out of the car and headed inside. It took my eyes a minute to adjust to the dark. A greeter in a black suit and a tiny moustache stepped up to me with a tight smile on his face.

I cleared my throat. "Jack Palace. I'm meeting someone."

"Yes, of course. Right this way, Mr. Palace." The greeter's eyes flickered over to Vin. Then he turned and led us to a private table in a private party room at the back. The kitchen, with its door to the alley, was close. That was good in case we had to make a break for it.

We were about half an hour early, and we were the first ones there. A server poured us water and brought us bread and oil and vinegar. I sipped the water, ignored the bread, and settled in to wait.

We didn't have to wait long. About ten minutes later, four guys in suits piled into the party room. They all stood there glaring at me and Vin. Vin and I stood up. One of the guys stepped forward. "I'm going to have to pat you down."

"But we just met."

The man's face went sour. "I heard you were a comedian."

"I'm just a guy trying to make an honest living."

"Yeah. Us, too." The men guffawed. I stood up and slightly raised my hands. I had left my knives at home. If one of the suit boys wanted to make a move, now would be the time.

The man patted me down, nodded slightly, and turned to Vin. "You next."

Vin had left his gun in the car. He wasn't happy about it, but it was what it was. The man patted him down and turned to the others. "They're clean."

Two of the men left. Two of them stayed standing, watching us. I sat down and had another sip of water. Vin remained standing.

The two men came back, flanking a third. I knew in an instant it was DiAngelo. The man wasn't the sweatpants-wearing hothead I had heard about. He was older now, and wearing a suit. His hair was still slicked back, but it was turning silver at the temples. His face was tanned. Strangely, he was smiling.

"Jack," he said. "And you are —"

"Vin," said Vin.

"I gotta admit, Jack, this is a ballsy move. When Mario called me, at first I thought he was pulling my leg." DiAngelo pulled up a chair and sat down. Everyone else remained standing. DiAngelo turned to his crew. "Get you boys anything? Scotch? Some vino?" He turned back to me without waiting for an answer. He was still smiling, but his eyes were black and hard. "So, what are we doing here, Jack?"

"An associate of yours came to me recently with a proposition and a timeline."

DiAngelo nodded. "Yeah, yeah. I know all about it."

"If I do this thing for you, would you really let me go?"

DiAngelo sighed. He dragged a breadstick through the oil. "Jack, I'm a businessman. You know this. You, you're bad for business. Tommy, The Old Man's son — right about now he should be sitting on top of the world. Instead, he got mixed up with you. And where is he now?" He held up his hand. "Don't answer. That's one of those, whaddaya call it, rhetorical questions. We all know that wherever Tommy is, he ain't coming back."

"He saved my life, and I saved his. I paid my debt."

DiAngelo scowled. "Point is, he's still gone. And so is Freddy." DiAngelo leaned back. He pointed his half-eaten breadstick at me. "There was no love lost between me and Freddy. He ran his crew his way, and I run things my way. But Freddy, Tommy, they got around you and they stopped living. You see how that's a troublesome connection."

"I didn't kill Freddy."

"Maybe you didn't, but then again, maybe you did."

"Think about it, Sammy. Freddy was my friend. Why would I kill him?"

"Grover's your friend, too. Or so I hear."

There it was. The other shoe had dropped.

"He is my friend. You know I can't kill him."

"Yeah, I know." DiAngelo leaned back and exhaled loudly. "That whole cockamamie plan wasn't my idea. Can you believe that? Some associates of mine pitched it to me and I thought, yeah, sure, why not." He stared at me from across the table. I could feel Vin tense up behind me. "I got a surprise for you."

"I don't like surprises."

"You'll like this one." DiAngelo held up his hand and snapped his fingers. The back door opened. Two more goons came trooping in, followed by Butterface.

This is it, I thought. *I'm going to die.*

It was a calm feeling. I'd had this feeling before, years ago, when I was a young man. I'd had a disagreement with someone and ended up in the hospital. The other guy had ended up in the morgue. I'd thought I was on my way there, too. Ribs broken, arm broken, jaw broken. Left eye swollen shut. I hurt so bad I'd thought I was dying. As the doctors rushed around me in the ER, I felt a curtain of calm descend over me. Like, *I've done everything I can do. I made it to the hospital, and now it's out of my hands. If I die, I die.*

Vin stepped forward, his fists coming up. I grabbed his arm and pulled him back. I stood up. Who knew this would be how it all ended, sitting around a table eating breadsticks?

Butterface blinked. "Jack. What a surprise."

DiAngelo nodded slightly. One of the goons flanking Butterface hauled off and hit him in the back of the head with the butt of his gun. Butterface crumpled like a dropped accordion. The goon hit him again and again and again.

DiAngelo held up a hand. "All right, all right. That's enough."

The goon straightened up, breathing heavily. His face was flecked with Butterface's blood.

Vin looked at me and I looked at him. We were both thinking the same thing: *What the hell?*

DiAngelo was staring at me. "You know how I got to where I am today?"

By being a ruthless son of a bitch. "No, I don't."

"I followed the script. I didn't rock the boat. I did what I was told to do, and I did it with respect." DiAngelo pointed over at Butterface sprawled out on the party room floor. "That guy there, he's a loose cannon. Turns out he was stealing from me. He and the manager of this dump were skimming cash off the top. Can you believe that shit?" DiAngelo shook his head sadly. "Hard to find good help these days. So, now I've got an opening for a new manager. And also a new whatever that guy was. No, don't look like that. I'm not proposing you take the gig. You and I, we're more alike than you think. We're both loyal. I knew you were never going to kill Grover. I can respect that about you. He's still got to go, but that's for another day. And you ..." DiAngelo shrugged. "Mario vouches for you. I respect Mario. I'm loyal to Mario. Do you understand?"

I understood. I was alive because I had visited an old man and drunk his lemonade and eaten his cookies.

One of the goons gestured toward Butterface lying bleeding on the floor. "He's still breathing, boss."

DiAngelo glanced at me. "You want to do the honours?"

I shook my head. "I don't do that anymore."

DiAngelo grinned. "Look at that, boys. A real Boy Scout." He nodded at the goon standing over Butterface. "Finish it."

The goon screwed a silencer onto his gun. Two shots and the man was done.

The goons grabbed a tablecloth and started wrapping Butterface up. DiAngelo looked at me. "Your pal Grover. He's still gonna answer for Freddy. You go home and you think about where your loyalties lie."

CHAPTER 28

Vin and I didn't talk much on the drive back home. Something about seeing a man murdered right in front of you puts the kibosh on conversation. I wasn't sure what Vin was thinking, but I was thinking about my own mortality. That whole scene with DiAngelo had been too damn close for comfort. I made a mental note to send Mario the best damn fruit basket anyone had ever seen. A mountain of apples and oranges and mangos with sparklers shooting out the top. Something.

Vin glanced over at me. "Grover is fucked."

"Maybe. He's been fucked before, but somehow he always gets unfucked."

"Sooner or later his luck is going to run out."

I raised my eyebrow. "You thinking about that price on his head?"

"What? No, man! C'mon, Jack. You know me."

"It's a lot of money, that's all."

Vin grunted. "Fuck the money."

"What, you're allergic to money now?" I grinned. "Everyone likes money."

Vin shot me the side-eye. "Now you're just fucking with me."

"Guilty as charged."

We headed back to Chinatown. I felt light, almost giddy. Escaping death can do that to a man. Now I could talk to Suzanne, tell her she didn't have to leave. The Chief's old land would be sold, and soon I'd have a basket of cash. Together Suzanne and I could blow through town and head out to greener pastures. Sit on the porch of that fabled cabin in the woods.

Suddenly I sat forward. Vin looked over at me. "You okay?"

"Yeah. Just thinking, is all." Maybe there was another player in this game. DiAngelo had folded on my hit pretty quick. These "associates" DiAngelo had spoken of. Maybe Butterface had been acting on their behalf.

In this business, you make a lot of enemies. It's just the nature of the beast. I thought back to what Bobby had told me in Freddy's old joint on the Danforth. *Everyone's got a price on their head. Cost of doing business.*

There was no love lost between me and Bobby, that was for sure. The man had tried to kill me, and I'd been forced to fight back. Maybe I had even killed his buddy — I had beaten him pretty badly — but if I had killed him, it had been self-defence. Those were the kinds of things I told myself to help me sleep at night. Problem was, it didn't really work.

Grover was planning to hit the counting house. What if it wasn't DiAngelo's? What if it was really owned by his "associates," whoever they were? Then hitting the house would open up a new world of trouble. I had to tell him. "I need to find Grover."

"That guy's bad news, Jack."

"We're all bad news. Do you know anyone who's good news?"

Vin thought for a while. "Eddie's daughter. Dawn."

I had to give him that one. Somehow Eddie had done a bang-up job compartmentalizing his life. He kept his wife and child — grown-up child, now, but she would always be Eddie's baby — out of his business.

We turned south on Spadina. The crowds pushed along the sidewalks. The signs started changing from English to Chinese. We were getting close to home.

Home. That box-filled office was as close to a real home as I'd ever had. Even when I was camping out in The Chief's trailer, it was my office that I thought of whenever I thought of home. It would be hard to leave, but everything has to end sometime. And it wasn't like I was going to torch the place before I left. I could always come back to visit, and I would.

We pulled into the alley. I glanced over at him. "Thanks for coming with me."

Vin exhaled. "Man, that was some fucked-up shit."

"Yeah."

"Well," Vin said, "my day can only go up from here."

"Shit, man. Don't say that. Don't tempt the gods."

"You a pantheist now, Jack?"

"A what?"

"Someone who believes in lots of gods."

"It's just, you know, a figure of speech. Don't tempt fate. You like that better?"

"It's all a bunch of superstition to me. I never did believe in that stuff." Vin grinned. "Cash on the barrelhead. That's my god."

"I thought you didn't like money." I grinned at him. "If you see Grover, let him know I'm looking for him."

"If I see Grover, I'm going to run the other way." Vin laughed. "See ya around, Jack."

I went up to my office. I gave the plant some water, then I sat there among the boxes. I had thought about maybe helping Eddie move these boxes somewhere else, but forget about it. I wouldn't be here that much longer. I pulled out my phone and called Suzanne.

"It's me. Don't hang up."

"Why would I hang up?"

"I don't know, I thought maybe you were mad at me. You know, that whole 'get out of town' thing."

"I am still mad at you. Get out of town — why don't you get out of town?"

"I've got some good news. I had a little crisis there, but I think it's over."

"Until next time."

"With any luck, there won't be a next time. Start looking for cabins, babe." There was silence at the other end. "Suzanne? Hello?"

"I'm here. Jack, you can't jerk me around like this."

"What do you mean?"

"One minute you're telling me to flee for my life and the next minute you're telling me to start hanging up curtains. I'm getting whiplash over here."

"Sorry, sorry. I'm just trying —"

"Yeah, yeah, I know. You're trying to keep me safe."

"What can I say? That's what I want." I still thought Suzanne would be safer out of town and away from me, at least for a couple more days. December was right around the corner. With any luck, we could spend Christmas together without having to constantly check over our shoulders. Santa coming down the chimney and not a hit man with a gun in his hand.

"Are you for real about the cabin?"

"I am. As real as it gets." Suddenly I felt cold. "Are you?"

"Am I for real about the cabin?"

"Yeah."

She hesitated, about three beats too long. "I think so. It's hard, you know? You and I … maybe we're better as a fantasy."

"We can make this fantasy a reality."

"And then what? We sit around arguing about who has to take out the trash?"

"It doesn't have to be that way."

"Doesn't it?" She paused. "I think back to every stupid little argument Steve and I ever had, and I just want to kick myself. Life is short, you know? Life is so damn short."

"It is. Let's make the most of it while we can."

Suzanne sighed. "The cabin."

"The cabin."

"All right, I'll start looking."

I hung up the phone. The call had ended well, but I was still a little unsettled. Was she having second thoughts? Was I? Was it actually possible for me to change my life?

I went out walking. The Chinatown crowds swirled around me. Grocers stacked lettuce and rearranged piles of oranges. Empty produce boxes were heaped on the curb. It was around four in the afternoon, and the sun was already setting. It was cold and getting colder. I ducked into a store and bought a pair of gloves. It was still dark and cold, but at least my hands were warm.

I found myself in front of the bar. *C'mon, Jack. Just one drink. Maybe a beer. Just a beer.* What's the harm in that?

I heard Eddie's voice in my head. *You know beer has alcohol in it, right?* Was I in or was I out? Was I really quitting drinking, or was I just spinning my wheels? As Big Daddy Kane said, ain't no half-steppin'. Was I serious about wanting to lead a new life, or not?

I stared at the bar door and then I kept on walking.

CHAPTER 29

The forty-eight-hour deadline came and went. Butterface didn't rise from the dead. I was still alive and well, and as far as I knew, so was Grover.

The deadline might've passed, but I didn't feel like I was out of the woods just yet. Having Butterface killed right in front of me had been a weird show of force that was a message of some kind. I didn't think DiAngelo had done it out of the kindness of his heart, or out of loyalty to Mario. Oh sure, maybe some of it was because of Mario, but DiAngelo could've iced Butterface at any place and any time. He didn't have to do it right in front of me. That had been a message, for sure. Betray me, fuck with me, and this is what you get.

But was the message for me or Grover? With any luck, Grover was lying low right now. Deep cover was the name of the game. DiAngelo was still gunning for Grover and maybe for me, too.

Or maybe I was just paranoid. I rubbed my eyes. Tired, man. It was hard to think straight.

"Psst. Jack."

My head snapped up. Grover was standing by my office window.

"You know, I wish you wouldn't do that."

"What?"

"The whole appearing in my office out of nowhere thing."

Grover frowned. "Don't look so happy to see me."

"DiAngelo's still gunning for you. He killed Butterface right in front of me. I mean, he had one of his goons do it, but it was a message all the same."

"Message? What message?"

"He's going to kill you out of loyalty to Freddy. At least, I think that was the gist."

Grover laughed. "I swear, Jack. These guys and their vendettas. Don't get me wrong, I understand. I've gone off all half-cocked on crusades before. Maybe there's something about this lifestyle that appeals to obsessive types. Who knows? I'm not a doctor." His whole face suddenly changed. His eyes darkened, and he scowled. "I was supposed to kill Butterface, though. Me."

"He's dead and gone, Grover. Let it go."

"I'm hitting that counting house. You want in? Mucho dinero, my friend. Mucho, mucho."

"It might not DiAngelo's."

"Say what?"

"The counting house. It might not be his. There's other players in this game."

"Who?"

"DiAngelo's associates. Could be top-level guys."

"Well, shit. There's a fly in the ointment." Grover frowned. "I can't knock over the counting house if I don't know who it belongs to. I mean, come on. You know I'm a patient guy, Jack, but I can't be watching that damn house 24-7." He kept scowling at me as if the counting house possibly not belonging to Sammy was somehow my fault.

"So it'll take some time. With Butterface out of the picture, that's time we've got."

Grover grinned. "Does that mean you're in?"

Retirement. Enough money to fuck right off. Sit on the porch with Suzanne and not worry about paying the bills. "We've got to figure out who the house belongs to first. An operation like that …"

"Oh, it's big, Jack. Money flows into that apartment house like water down the Nile."

"So we're not dealing with small-timers here."

Grover's hands twitched. He made a fist and then unclenched it. I could tell he wanted to leave my office and hit the house right then and there. "Fuck it. Whoever it is, we're going to take that money. We'll figure out whose money it is and then we'll take it. I'm going to see a few people, put a team together. You in?"

"Depending on whose money it is …"

"Yeah?"

"Yeah. I'm in."

CHAPTER 30

It was around midnight. Grover and I sat in his car and watched the apartment building. This time of night, not too many people were going in or out. People were still walking by, though, on their way to the Roncesvalles bars. Getting all boozed up, grabbing some late-night eats, aw yeah. I'd have been lying if I said I didn't miss it.

"Who do you think it is?" Grover kept peering at the apartment building. "Sammy DiAngelo and his associates ... 'Associates' covers a lot of ground."

"All we know for sure is that Butterface dropped off money here. And more people keep dropping off money, a lot of money. Where do you think it's all coming from?"

"All over the damn place. Construction, gambling, prostitution, drugs."

I stared at the building. Lights were on in various units. "You say the cash is on the third floor?"

"That's right. They drop off the cash in a unit on the second floor. Someone else trucks the cash upstairs to the counting house. They've got machines going around the clock. We're talking millions."

"And when you were watching the building, who was doing the pickups?"

Grover shook his head. "I couldn't tell. It's not like anyone was walking out with giant sacks with dollar signs." He shifted, still keeping his eyes on the building. "Near as I can tell, most of the cash goes into the safe."

"You said you creeped the room. What's the safe look like?"

"I won't lie, the safe looks like a son of a bitch. Maybe I can crack it, but then again, maybe I can't." Grover grinned. "Luckily, I know someone who can."

"Let's not get ahead of ourselves. We've got to figure out who's running this show. We don't want to bite off more than we can chew."

"Cliché city, Jack."

"Yeah, well, clichés are clichés for a reason." I sat back against the leather seats. "I don't think we're going to find out anything else tonight."

Grover peered out the window. "Drugs." He sounded disgusted. "Did I ever tell you about my sister?"

"No." I had never heard Grover talk about his family, ever.

"She's three years younger than me. Lives out in Vancouver. She's a heroin addict. She shoots up two hundred, three hundred dollars a day. That's nine thousand dollars a month. One hundred and eight thousand dollars a year. That's good money, Jack. Damn good money that she just flushes away." He looked over at me. "She's overdosed eight times that

I know of. Once she died on the operating table. You hear me? She was fucking dead and then they revived her and she came back to life. The dealers. They got their hooks into her and that's that. She deals herself now. That's how she can afford the shit." Grover sat quietly for a minute.

"It started out with pills. The doctors prescribed her that shit, can you believe it? The drug companies flat-out lied and said their shit wasn't addictive. 'Oh, these pills full of opioids? Oh, yeah, they're slow release, so you know, don't worry about it. Slow release means you won't get hooked. Fucking bullshit." He ran his hand through his hair. "She got addicted and no joke. When the pills ran out, she bought them on the street. But that shit's expensive as hell. Twenty, thirty bucks a pill. Heroin's a whole lot cheaper." He straightened up. "Dealers. Fuck them." He smiled. "We're going to take their shit. You and me and my guys, we're going to march right on in there and take it all."

"This is a big operation. There's big people behind it."

"So we plan it carefully. Leave nothing to chance."

Leave nothing to chance. It was a nice thought, but we were dealing with people here. Maybe they'd go along with Grover's plan, but more likely they would fight back. I wasn't up for murder, no matter how much money was involved.

"Don't look like that, Jack. There's two people in there at any given time. Three, tops. We go in — you, me, the safecracker, and two other guys — we've got it all covered. We go in fast with the element of surprise on our side. In and out, nobody gets hurt."

Grover fired up the engine. We drove east on Dundas, back toward Chinatown. It was time for my head to hit the pillow.

"Grover, don't do anything until we figure a few more things out."

"Don't worry." The little man smiled. "You think I'm a mad, methed-out stickup boy? We'll do our research. Don't you worry about that."

He pulled up in front of Eddie's building. We said our goodnights and then I went inside. I thought about going down to the casino, but instead I headed directly to bed. I prayed that sleep would come easy. Tomorrow was another day.

CHAPTER 31

I woke up to someone ringing my doorbell. I made sure to grab a knife before I went downstairs and peered through the peephole in the door leading out to the street. Grover was standing there with a big frown on his face.

I unlocked the door and pushed it open. "You're using the doorbell now?"

"You said to stop just showing up. You think I don't listen? I listen, Jack. I listen and I learn."

"Come on up." I glanced sideways at the little man. "You get any sleep?"

"Not yet. I went back to the apartments."

"What's up?"

Grover plopped down on my couch. "You got any Scotch?"

"It's nine o'clock in the morning."

"It's okay, I've been up all night."

"Sorry."

"All right, forget about it. So I went back to the apartments. I saw a guy go in with a duffle bag full of cash. The guy was Salvatore Ricci. I know for a fact that guy works for Sammy DiAngelo."

"So it's either Sammy's own counting house or his boss's."

"Yep. Salvatore is a solid soldier." Grover patted his pockets. "Got any cigarettes?"

"Since when do you smoke?"

"I only smoke when I'm tired."

"That shit will kill you, Grover. Lung cancer."

"There's other kinds of cancer, too."

"What?"

"They're bad for you. I get it. It's not like I smoke a pack a day." Grover waved his hand. "Forget about it. I'm going to go crash for a little bit. Then we need to get back up on the apartments."

"You don't need me for that."

Grover scowled. "You already hanging me out to dry?"

"No, nothing like that. I just think I could do some legwork, you know, ask around about the apartments. See if anyone knows anything."

"Nix to that. Start spreading the word about the apartments and that shit will blow back on us once the deal goes down. 'Oh, the counting house got hit? Yeah, Jack was asking about that a few weeks ago.' You see how that works?"

I hated to admit it, but the little man was right. "Let me ask Eddie. Just Eddie."

"And Eddie asks a guy who asks a guy. The whole freakin' switchboard lights up. It's no good, Jack. We gotta play our cards close to the vest."

"All right, all right." I nodded at him. "Have a nice rest."

Grover shook my hand and walked out. He was handling the counting house with the same level of obsession he brought to all his capers. Not for the first time, I wondered if I was an idiot for getting involved. All that money, though. Retirement beckoned. I didn't need a solid-gold house or a rocket car, just enough to support Suzanne and myself. The money from The Chief's land sale would help, but it wouldn't be enough on its own.

I sat among the boxes and I thought. The obvious reason why one of DiAngelo's guys was going into the counting house was because the counting house was DiAngelo's. But that still didn't rule out the faceless associates.

Money from a lot of different operations flowed into the counting house, then flowed out to get laundered. The cash would get mixed into legitimate cash-heavy businesses like bars and restaurants. It would come out of the till clean as a whistle. DiAngelo could declare that shit on his taxes and look like a legitimate businessman.

I stood up and poured the plant some water. I didn't want to overwater it, but I didn't want it to die, either. My phone rang, vibrating on the desktop. I picked it up.

"Hello?"

"Jack! It's Kevin Rhodes."

"What's up, Kevin?"

"Good news, my friend. The deal's gone through. The land's been sold."

"How much?"

"Right down to it, eh? A hundred and fifty thousand. Minus my commission, of course."

The price seemed low to me, but raw land with only a falling-apart barn on it was never going to equal the price of land plus a house. Plus there was the location, out in the middle of nowhere. That amount of land in the city would be worth millions.

"I'll take it." The one-fifty would cover a nice cabin in the woods. Then we'd need operating income. Or a nice little nest egg. The counting house could cover that.

DiAngelo's counting house, or his associates'? Either way, there something was screwy with DiAngelo. Even with Mario's help, I didn't figure he'd let me skate that easily. Something was up, but I didn't know what. Not knowing was making me nervous.

I ended the call with Kevin Rhodes and went down to the casino. It was fairly quiet this early in the morning. There were a few grinders doing their thing at the poker tables. From the looks of it, they had been there all night long.

Eddie was perched on his usual barstool. He had big black circles under his eyes. "What's the good word, Jack?"

"I sold The Chief's land. Got some cash coming my way."

"Good for you." He pointed to Vivian. "Set my man up with the finest club soda in the house. We're celebrating."

Vivian grinned and poured me a Perrier. I wasn't actually too crazy about the stuff. To me it tasted like melted rocks. Too many damn minerals. Still, I toasted Eddie and we drank.

Eddie frowned and leaned in close. "There's a guy standing over by the door. Tall guy in a suit. You know him?"

My eyes flickered over to the door. The man looked familiar, but I couldn't place him. "Maybe?"

"He's coming over."

Eddie let his hand dangle near his stomach. I knew that beneath his suit jacket, he had a gun. I let my own hand creep closer to the knife beneath my jacket. The tall man came up to us and nodded. "Jack. Eddie."

Eddie squinted. "Do I know you?"

The tall man smiled. "No, not really. The name's Nico. I work for a mutual friend."

"Oh yeah? Or maybe you work for the cops. What do you think, Jack? Doesn't this guy look like a cop?"

"There's all kinds of cops, Eddie."

"Yeah, and this guy's one of them. What do you want, man? I'm all paid up here." I had seen Eddie pay off the cops before. A big thick envelope changed hands and then the cops went on their merry way. It happened every week, but I'd only seen it that one time.

Nico smiled an uneasy smile. "You busting my balls or what? I'm not a fucking cop."

Eddie held up his hands. "All right, all right. So maybe you're legit. Maybe you're not. Are you here to play poker or what?"

"I'm just here to talk to Jack."

Eddie turned to me and winked. "Whaddaya say, Jack? You want to talk to the cop?"

I nodded. "Sure, why not? What can I do for you?"

"The man wants to see you."

"Who? DiAngelo?" Nico nodded. I frowned. "I don't have any business with him. Not anymore."

Nico held up his hands. "You'll have to talk to him. I'm just the messenger."

"Let me guess. I get in your car, right? I sit up front. There's a guy sitting behind me. We start to drive, and all of a sudden a wire slices through my throat. Is that about it?"

"He's got a business proposition for you."

"An offer I can't refuse?"

"Refuse it or not, fuck, I don't care."

"All right, where's he want to meet? I'll take my own car, if it's all the same to you."

The tall man gave me the address of a club on King Street West. I grinned. "That's a swanky club. Do I get bottle service? Can I bring a date?"

Nico grinned and patted me on the shoulder. "You're a funny guy. We'll see you tonight."

Eddie and I watched the tall man go. He turned to me. "What the fuck was that all about?"

"Who knows?" I sipped my rock water. "I guess I'll find out tonight."

"I think Vin is busy. You want me to come along?"

"Nah. Sammy didn't kill me yesterday, so he probably won't kill me today."

Eddie raised his eyebrows. "That's a dangerous way to think, Jack. It's like those ads for mutual funds. They always say 'past performance is no guarantee of future results.'"

I finished my drink. "That's good advice. See you around, Eddie."

"Yeah, man. I hope so."

CHAPTER 32

The King West scene was hopping. Girls wearing silver coats and way-too-short skirts shivered in the cold. Guys with gold chains and slicked-back hair high-fived each other. A cop on a horse trotted by.

A bouncer who looked like a shaved gorilla put out his hand as I tried to enter Sammy's club. "Back of the line, pal."

"I'm meeting DiAngelo."

The bouncer stared at me. I stared right back. "Name?"

"Name's Jack. Jack Palace."

The bouncer murmured something into his earpiece. We waited in the cold. A limo drove by, girls shrieking from the sunroof. "Yeah, all right. Go on in."

"Thanks." I nodded to the bouncer and headed inside. The old me would've said something snarky to try to put the bouncer in his place. The new, mellow me knew that the guy was just trying to do his job.

Inside, the music was pumping. The bass felt like I was being kicked in the chest. A DJ was dancing on a platform about twenty feet over the dance floor. Getting paid big bucks to press play on his laptop. It was working, though: the crowd was going nuts. A sea of humanity rose and fell. Outside it was below freezing, but in here it was humid and tropical from the heat and sweat of the dancers' bodies.

I walked up the stairs to a VIP area. The tall man from earlier was lounging against the wall just inside the VIP room. I shook his hand. "Nico, right?"

"You got it, Jack. Follow me."

He led me through the VIP area and into a small backroom. Cases of booze were stacked to the ceiling. There was a table in the middle of the room and about six chairs. Nico pulled out a chair for me. I hesitated. The sound from the dance floor was muffled in here, but the club was so loud a hit man wouldn't even need a silencer. I could get my head blown off right here and no one would hear a thing.

"Go on, have a seat. Mr. DiAngelo will be right in."

I sat down. I looked at the cases of booze. A few months back, this would've been my fantasy. Booze to the ceiling. An ocean of booze.

The door opened, and DiAngelo and two goons walked in. I recognized the goon on the left. He was the guy who killed Butterface back at the café. My heart galloped. Was tonight my turn?

I stood up. DiAngelo shook my hand. "Thanks for coming down, Jack. I appreciate it."

"Well, you know. You're more or less in the neighbourhood." In fact I had walked here, straight down Spadina into clubland.

I wasn't buying DiAngelo's nice guy act for a second. Thanks for coming down? I appreciate it? He was pulling the catch-more-flies-with-honey trick on me, and it was making me nervous.

He tilted his chin toward the chair directly across from him. "Go on, have a seat. Can I get you a drink?"

"I don't drink. Not anymore."

"A soda pop, then. Coca-Cola? Chocolate milk?"

The goon who killed Butterface snickered. I wanted to pick up a chair and hit him with it. Instead, I glared at him and sat back down. "A Coke sounds good."

DiAngelo glanced at Nico. He snapped to it, heading out the door, and was back in a minute, putting the bubbly soft drink down in front of me.

DiAngelo waited until I'd had a sip, then he leaned in. "Let me cut right to it, Jack. We could use a man of your talents."

I raised my left eyebrow. "Does that mean you don't want me dead anymore?"

"Who said I wanted you dead?" DiAngelo spread his hands wide. "I know you've heard things about me. And I can guess that some of those things, they weren't that nice. But I'm on the level here. Lester, he thought you and Grover were on the outs. He thought either you would kill him, or he would kill you. Either way, it would have been pure gravy for us. Me, I knew otherwise. You still think Grover's your buddy. You're a loyal guy — there's no way you're going to kill your buddy. I can understand that. And I can appreciate that. That's the kind of loyalty I like to see." He leaned closer. "The price on your head, that didn't come from me. Sure, I went along with it because I'm a loyal guy, too. But I'm here to tell you this: you work for me, the price on your head goes away."

Suzanne, I thought. Her and me, safe in our little cabin in the woods. "Work for you, huh?"

DiAngelo leaned back with a satisfied smirk on his face. "I'm not asking you to do anything crazy here. You do for me what you did for Tommy. You work collections. Pick up some money, drop it off. Easy peasy."

"And if they don't pay?"

DiAngelo kept smirking. "That, my friend, is entirely up to you."

The goon who killed Butterface stepped closer. Nico stood by the door, watching my face intently. I got the feeling this wasn't an offer I could refuse.

"I run your routes and the price on my head goes away."

"That's about the size of it. You're a smart guy, Jack. Whaddaya say?"

I took a sip of Coke and stared DiAngelo right in the eyes. "I'll do it."

CHAPTER 33

"You made a deal with the devil." Grover frowned and paced back and forth across my office floor. "It's a bad move, Jack. This guy gets his hooks in you, he's never gonna let you go."

"What I did is buy us some time."

Grover whirled. "Bullshit. You bought yourself some time. I'm still twisting in the wind here. I've still got a price on my head. You really think the contract on you didn't come from DiAngelo? Bullshit, bullshit, bullshit. He's going to kill you, Jack. He's luring you into a false sense of security and then he's going to kill us both." Grover stepped closer to me. His face twisted into an angry grimace. His eyes were burning. "There's only one thing we can do here. We knock over the counting house. We snatch all his money, then we kill that sonofabitch ourselves."

I stared at him. "Do you think I'm a fool?"

"C'mon, Jack —"

"No. Do you think I'm a fool? I know DiAngelo can't be trusted. Sending Butterface to try to get you and me to kill each other, that's classic DiAngelo. When he realized it wasn't going to work, he cut his losses, killed Butterface, and switched tactics. He's acting all lovey-dovey now, but I know it's all bullshit. Keep your friends close and your enemies closer. He wants to keep me in his back pocket and use me before I'm killed. Believe me, I get it."

"The only way out of this is for us to kill him first."

"Say that's true. I don't believe it is, but let's say for the sake of argument that it is. Wouldn't it be better if I was working from the inside? DiAngelo wants to keep me close, fine. I'll be close enough to slit his throat."

Grover coughed and kept coughing. I walked to the bathroom and got him a glass of water. He drank it down and wiped his mouth with a lavender handkerchief.

"You okay?"

He waved my concern away. "Don't worry about it. You talk a good game. How do I know you're not just telling me what I want to hear?"

I took his empty water glass and set it down on the desk next to my plant. "This shit right here, this is exactly what DiAngelo wants. He wants us at each other's throats. He says he'll take the price off my head but keeps it on yours. Why? To make you paranoid and suspicious of me. And look, it's working."

Grover sank down into my couch and sat there in silence. The man looked smaller than usual. Finally, he raised his head and smiled. "You're right, Jack. I've been acting like a grade-A jackass."

"Don't worry about it. We all have our moments."

Grover grinned. "So now you're working for DiAngelo."

"For now."

"We can turn this to our advantage."

"Hell, yeah, we can."

"If you're making collections, maybe some of that cash will flow to the counting house. That could be our in."

"Could be." I sipped my own water. "We'll find out tomorrow. I'm running a route with my new pal Nico."

"Nico, huh?" Grover stood up. "Try not to get killed."

"That's the plan."

CHAPTER 34

It was a dangerous game I was playing. Sure, I had bought myself some time, but I had also walked willingly into the belly of the beast.

Nico picked me up at around ten in the morning. Ten was early for a gangster. Most gangsters I knew liked to stay up late partying and then sleep in the next day. I knew a guy who'd worked security for a candy company down in Mexico City. The delivery trucks would deliver the candy to the corner stores, and it was basically a cash and carry business. They had to roll through some pretty rough neighbourhoods, and sure enough, the trucks were getting knocked over left, right, and centre. What my buddy the security guy did was to get them to change the time of the deliveries. The trucks started rolling through in the early morning instead of the afternoon. The robberies dropped off because all the gangsters were still sleeping.

Nico, though, he looked wide awake. He smiled at me as I slid into his car. It was totally clean and it still smelled new. Hell, for all I knew, it was new. "New car?"

"We switch 'em out every now and then. You know how it is."

"Sure."

"Look, Jack, I know you probably still have reservations about this whole thing. But let me tell you, Sammy's not the demon that other people make him out to be. Deep down, he's a pretty decent guy."

"Good to know," I said. I thought about Butterface — Lester — being beaten to a pulp right in front of me on DiAngelo's nod.

We drove down to Queen Street West and then we headed west toward Parkdale. We passed Tibetan shops and Tibetan restaurants. Not for the first time, I wondered why so many Tibetans had decided that Parkdale was the place to be. There was a big Buddhist temple in the neighbourhood, but which had come first, the temple or the people?

We pulled into a parking spot right in front of one of Parkdale's many bars. Nico looked over at me and grinned. "This is it. You coming?"

I nodded. This early, the bar was closed, but Nico knocked twice and the door was unlocked. A man ducked behind the bar and I tensed up, half expecting him to come back up with a shotgun. Instead, he came up with a manila envelope stuffed with cash. Nico slid it into his inside jacket pocket and then we were back out on the street. He looked over at me and smiled. "You see? Easy like snapping."

Some people don't know how to snap, I wanted to say, but I figured it was best to keep quiet.

The morning went like that. We went into bars and restaurants, they gave us envelopes full of cash. I wasn't sure if it was protection money or from gambling or drugs or what, but all the envelopes went into Nico's jacket, then into the glovebox of his car. I was more or less just along for the ride.

I was hoping that at any minute, we would head toward Roncesvalles and the counting house. Hopefully I'd get to walk up with Nico and take a good long look at the place. Grover had creeped it once, but I wanted to look for any strengths and weaknesses with my own eyes. How many guys were inside? What kind of safe were they storing the money in? The more information we had, the better.

Only we didn't go to the counting house. We went back to that same liquor-filled storeroom in DiAngelo's King Street club. Nico and I had transferred the envelopes out of the glovebox and into a briefcase. He slid the briefcase across the table to DiAngelo, who didn't even bother opening it. DiAngelo glanced at me and then looked at Nico. "Any trouble?"

"No trouble."

DiAngelo turned his steel-grey eyes onto me. "What did I tell you? The operation runs as smooth as silk."

Nico patted my back. "Same time tomorrow. I'll see you then."

I walked back to Eddie's building from King Street. My head was buzzing with confusion. I didn't like that feeling one bit.

They didn't need me to run these routes. DiAngelo was showing off. But why? Maybe he was just one of those guys who was pathological about the need to prove himself. My suit is more expensive than yours, my car is more expensive, my shoes, my haircut. Maybe DiAngelo had a micropenis and this whole thing was about over-compensation. Who knows?

Suzanne was waiting for me down in the casino. The action at the poker tables was hot and heavy today. The woman poker player was back, and once again she was cleaning house. Her chip stack was growing by the minute. I'd asked Eddie once why he used poker chips when every other illegal casino I knew about was strictly cash and carry, money on the table, not chips. He looked at me and said, "Same reason I have a roulette wheel. No one goes to a fucking illegal casino to play roulette. But I wanted the place to look real."

The chips, the suits, the wheel — it was all part of the same grand illusion. In the same way, DiAngelo was working some kind of sleight-of-hand illusion on me. I just hadn't figured it out yet.

Suzanne kissed my cheek. "You get any sleep?"

"Surprisingly, yeah. I slept pretty well. You?"

"I was thinking about you last night."

"Oh yeah?"

"Yeah." She kissed me on the lips and lightly bit my lower lip. "Cabin in the woods, no cabin in the woods. It doesn't matter, Jack. I want us to be together."

We left the casino and headed up to my office. This time, we took our time. She pushed me gently down to the couch and then stood in front of me, swaying slightly to music only she could hear. She unbuttoned her shirt slowly, button by button, staring at me the whole time. I started to rise but she wagged her finger and shook her head. She slid her shirt off and tossed it to me on the couch. She was dancing now, her hips swaying as she reached behind her back and unfastened her bra. Her breasts sprang free. She pinched her dark-pink nipples. I started to get up again, and this time she pushed me back, gently but firmly. She undid the top button of her pants, unzipped them, and pulled down the fabric, flashing me a glimpse of her lacy black panties. She wriggled out of her pants and stood there, still swaying, wearing nothing but that lacy black thong. She turned her back and her butt to me, then smiled over her shoulder.

I couldn't take it anymore. I jumped off the couch and grabbed her ass with both hands. She yelped and then laughed. I moved my hands to her front, one hand closing around her right breast and the other hand cupping the front of her crotch. She moaned and stepped back, pressing her body into mine.

I tugged off my own pants. I yanked at her panties, but she grabbed onto them and held on tight. "Take everything off," she said. So I did. Once I was naked, I peeled down her panties slowly, the top of her dark pubic patch coming into view, followed by her pussy lips. I traced them with my fingertip, then I pushed my finger inside. She moaned again and dropped to her knees. She took me inside her warm wet mouth and began to move. I held her head lightly and rocked with her, pushing against her tongue.

Then she stood up and stepped over to the couch. She sat down and spread her legs. She looked at me with half-lidded eyes. I didn't need further invitation. I dropped down and began to lick her. She was salty, and she was sweet. She twisted, moaning, then she grabbed my head and pushed me closer. I licked faster, flicking my tongue all around her clit. Then I licked the clit itself and her back arched like she had been hit by lightning.

I swung her legs onto the couch and then I slowly pushed inside, filling her up. She gasped, and I gasped, too. She felt so good. I started out slow, then went a little bit faster, then faster, and then I couldn't control myself any longer. I plowed into her and she groaned and bit my shoulder.

She came before I did, shaking all over. I wasn't far behind. I pumped inside of her for what seemed like days. Spent, together we tumbled to the couch and lay there, our sweaty limbs entwined.

For a while, there was nothing but our heartbeats. Slowly, slowly, the world returned. I stroked her hair, and she smiled. Goddamn, she was beautiful.

"I know who you are, Jack," she whispered. "I know who you are and I don't care."

CHAPTER 35

She accepted me. But after she left, I started thinking. *I know who you are and I don't care.* I was violent, she knew that. I had hurt people, and I had killed people. I told myself it was only in self-defence, but I'd gotten myself into situations where I knew I would have to fight back. She didn't care.

That wasn't what she meant, though. Right? There was some judgment there. She knew I wasn't a good person, but she didn't care. Or maybe she saw there was still some small scrap of goodness left in me after all. I rubbed my forehead. Ever since I'd quit drinking, I was thinking too much. It gave me headaches.

I stood up and went down to the casino. The poker lady was gone, taking her winnings with her. Eddie sat smoking at the bar. He saw me and hastily put the cigarette out.

I didn't say anything. I just sat down beside him and patted him on the back. Vivian put a glass of club soda in front of me. The bubbles rose and fell.

Eddie smiled sheepishly. "It's not like I smoke all the time. It's been a tough week, that's all. I'm not really smoking again."

I spread out my hands. "Hey, I didn't say anything."

"Somehow that makes it worse. C'mon, bust my balls a little."

"There's always going to be a reason to do something. It's my birthday, it's my friend's birthday, it's fucking Arbour Day. You want to smoke? Go ahead and smoke. You don't need an excuse."

Eddie shook his head. "Fuck that. I don't want to smoke. It's just — the cravings, Jack. Sometimes the cravings are just too much."

I stared down at my glass of club soda. "I know what you mean." I looked over at him and grinned. "You gotta stay strong, though. I know you can do it."

Eddie smiled back. "It's back to the lollipops for me."

"Good. You still have a couple boxes of 'em upstairs."

"About that, you think it's time for me to clear out the old office or what?"

"Nah. I'm going to be gone soon. Taking my land sale money and getting the fuck out of Dodge."

Eddie kept smiling. "You're going to miss me, though. Your new place won't have a casino in the basement."

"Hell, I don't even gamble."

"You used to play cards."

"Yeah, I used to play a little poker every now and then. But then I started losing more often than I won, and the whole thing kind of lost its sparkle."

Eddie slid a slip of paper my way. "Grover called while you were upstairs. He wants you to call him at this number."

I stepped into Eddie's office and punched the number into my phone.

"Jack. The wheels are turning. I'm coming to pick you up."

"What's up?"

"We're going to talk to a buddy of mine."

In the car, Grover smiled at me. "You'll like this guy, Jack. Max Morris is his name. He's an old-school safe-cracker. This fucker can get into anything. All we need to do is convince him that this counting house job is a good one, and he's in."

We drove east. Max Morris lived in the Beaches, near Woodbine Beach. He had a little house on a quiet street. He gave Grover a hearty handshake at the door and showed us into a living room jam-packed with furniture and stuff. The whole room was a riot of cushions, pillows, stuffed animals, and cuckoo clocks. Max stood in the doorway to the kitchen and said, "Get you guys anything? Coffee? Tea? Cookies?"

Grover frowned. "You got anything stronger, Max?"

Max shook his head. "I gave all that up. You want a non-alcoholic beer?"

"Water's fine."

We sat among the clutter and sipped our water. Outside the living room window, a dog walker went by in a blizzard of legs and leashes. The dog walker's face was almost invisible beneath his huge puffy parka and black toque pulled down low. A light snow was falling.

Max pointed to a big cardboard box on the other side of the room. "I pulled out the Christmas stuff the other day. Now all I gotta do is get a tree. I got allergies, but my wife, she likes real trees. So, we'll get a real one and I'll sneeze a bit. But you know what they say: happy wife, happy life."

"How is Maggie?"

"She's good, she's good. She wants to get a dog, but you know — allergies."

Grover leaned forward. "Listen, Max. We've got a job lined up and we could use your help."

Max shook his head. "Uh-uh. Not me, man. These days I'm walking the straight and narrow. Doing some consulting work for a security firm, you know, how to keep your shit safe. Working with some pretty big-name companies. Some of these companies, man, they think their shit don't stink until we come in and prove different."

Grover looked over at me. "Tell 'im about it, Jack."

"It's a counting house. Lots and lots of untraceable cash."

"Who are you guys ripping off?"

"A real piece of shit. This guy's tried to have us killed at least once that we know of." Grover grinned. "We figure he owes us."

Max looked interested. "And you say there's a safe."

"That's right. I didn't get a good look at it, but it's there. I'm telling you, this place is stuffed with the do-re-mi. Stacks of cash to the ceiling. Well, not the ceiling. I won't exaggerate. But enough lettuce for all of us to sit back and live a nice comfortable life."

Max gestured to the overstuffed living room. "I got that now."

I leaned forward. "Do you, though? You like working with those corporate guys? Or would you rather have enough cash in your account that you could tell them all to go fuck themselves?"

Grover nodded. "That's right. We're talking fuck-off money here. You tell them to fuck off, you go fuck off, whatever you want." He gestured to the snow falling outside. "Beach vacations. Get away from all this cold and grey and damp."

"I don't mind the winter. And the beach? I live like minutes from the beach. I like walking the boardwalk in the winter. It's just me, the joggers, the dog walkers. I sit on a bench and watch the waves roll in."

"You'd have more time for all of that if you weren't working. Just saying, is all." Grover stared over at him. "You still hit the casinos?"

"I still go every now and then. Maggie sets a limit and I play within it."

"How'd you do?"

"You know how it goes. Sometimes you win and sometimes you don't."

"I heard you were a bit behind."

"I owe a little. But my luck's gonna change."

"Yeah, it is. You take this money, you could pay off your debits with plenty left over."

Max cocked his head. I could tell he was thinking about it.

"These corporate guys. Do they ever let you get your hands dirty?"

"Sure. I bust into safes all the time. It's to demonstrate to the clients that they're not as secure as they think they are."

"So you've still got the touch, is what you're saying."

"Hell, yeah, I've still got the touch."

"Well, then, this safe shouldn't be a problem."

"It's not a problem for me."

"Then why are we still talking? Come on, Max. We get in, we get out. We get the loot. What do you say?"

"In and out."

"That's right."

"All right." Max smiled. His eyes were shining. "I'm in."

CHAPTER 36

Grover turned the wheel and sent the car gliding north. "There's one other guy we need to see. He lives out in Scarborough, near the zoo." He fiddled with the radio while we drove. The radio crackled and then came in clear. Soft jazz filled the car. "The next guy we're going to see is a construction expert. He got sent to prison on a tunnel job. I'm not talking an actual physical under-the-ground tunnel. I mean this guy punches through buildings. We're going to need him, too."

Dave McDonald was the construction guy's name. He lived in a little bungalow that was much more sparsely furnished than Max Morris's claustrophobic living room. Dave lived alone. Grover turned to me and said, "When Dave first moved in here, he had like a TV set and some lawn furniture set up in the living room and that was it. The place stayed that way for months. Finally he got tired of us all making fun of him and went out and bought a couch."

Dave led us out through the snow to the garage. It looked like a machine shop. The smell of oil hung in the air. There was every tool imaginable, all of them neatly hanging on the walls or inside big metal racks.

"We'll need Sawzalls on this job," Grover said. "We're going through drywall and who knows what else."

Dave nodded. "Sawzalls I've got. Do you have plans for the place?"

"Like blueprints?"

"Yeah. Schematics. Stuff like that."

"I can draw you a map from memory."

"Well," Dave said, "I guess that'll have to do."

Back in the car, back to the jazz. Grover turned on the wipers to sweep the snow from the windshield. He looked over at me and smiled. "It's always a good feeling when the team comes together."

"And you trust these guys?"

"As much as I trust anyone. I mean, Max has a gambling problem, and Dave likes male escorts, but we all have our vices, right? They're solid guys. We've worked together before. When Dave went to prison, he didn't say boo about anyone else. He stood up, Jack. What more could you ask for?"

My phone rang. I flipped it open. "Jack, it's Nico. Change of plans. I'm coming to pick you up."

"I'm not at home. Give me about forty-five minutes." I hung up the phone and glanced over at Grover. "Got to get back. Nico's coming to get me."

"He's coming to get you, huh?"

"Not in the coming-to-attack-me sense."

"That you know of."

"For God's sake, Grover. Don't you get tired being so paranoid all the time?"

"Honestly? Yes. It wears on a man, Jack. You know what I'm talking about."

I did. Every footstep, every door knock. You just never knew. "So what about DiAngelo?"

"One thing at a time, Jack. We'll deal with the counting house, and then we'll deal with DiAngelo." Grover stared at me. His eyes were like marbles. "I'm going to need your help for both."

"I can't just walk up to DiAngelo and slit his throat."

"Sure, you can. You've got knives, right? It's easier than you think."

"Even if I could, there's also the question of getting away. The man's never alone. I bet he brings his bodyguards into the bathroom when he takes a shit."

Grover laughed. "I'll take that bet." He leaned forward. "Seriously, though, the bathroom. That might be the right time to do it. Slit that sadistic fuck's throat right on the john." He checked his watch. "I'm going over to Roncesvalles. Gonna watch the apartment for a while."

"Drop me off first. Let's see what Nico wants."

"You know it's nothing good."

"Maybe he wants to take me out for frosty chocolate milkshakes."

We both laughed.

Grover dropped me off in front of my building — Eddie's building — and then he was on the road again. I knew Grover would sometimes watch a target for weeks, trying to get a sense of the rhythm of the place. In this case, we might not have weeks. Maybe Nico *was* coming for me because DiAngelo had gotten suspicious. Maybe someone in DiAngelo's organization had seen Grover and me camped out in the car, eyeballing the counting house. Maybe a lot of things. Really, it was pointless to speculate. The least I could do was be prepared.

I popped the locks to my office and went inside. The place smelled like cardboard. The plant was still on my desk. I missed my old plant, but nothing lasts forever.

I strapped on knives. I had brought two along for the meeting with Grover's crew, and now I strapped on some more. Ankle. Chest. A tiny one at my left wrist. I wanted to be ready for whatever Nico was going to throw at me.

Bristling with points, like a porcupine, I headed out into the snow.

Nico's Town Car eased to the curb, leaving tire tracks in the snowy street. I got in. The car smelled like spearmint. "Nico. What's up?"

"We've got a hold-out. The boss wants us to deal with it personally." Each job I said yes to was just pulling me in deeper. It felt like I was getting sucked down in quicksand.

I shook my head. "I don't do that kind of work. Not anymore." In my youth I had been a champion leg-breaker. The Chief had taught me well. After the first few, I hadn't even felt sorry for them anymore. There were actions and there were consequences. Borrowing money and not paying it back were the actions, me and my baseball bat were the consequences.

"DiAngelo asked for you specifically. Said there'd be a bonus in it for you."

I stared at Nico. "Not everyone can be bought."

He smiled. "DiAngelo sees it differently. Come on, Jack. You're alive, right? You owe us."

Fuck. DiAngelo was going to dangle the price on my head over me every chance he got. Claiming the shot had been called by someone else. And now only Big Daddy DiAngelo could protect me but only if I went along with his program. Fuck that. I shook my head. "No."

"Well, come along, at least. Stand in the background and look intimidating. You're good at that."

Shit. Shit, shit, shit. I pulled on my seatbelt. "Let's roll."

CHAPTER 37

We rolled out to a warehouse down near Cherry Beach. There was a great Asian supermarket nearby that I had been to a couple of times with Eddie. The soda pop aisle was my favourite. Shelves and shelves full of interesting sodas from around the world.

Nico and I got out of the car. His shoes and my boots crunched through the snow as we walked toward the warehouse. It didn't look like this warehouse had been used in years. The hair on the back of my neck was standing straight up. I inched closer to Nico and let my hand dangle near the knife in my belt. He looked up at me and smiled. "Why do you think some people don't pay their debts?"

"All kinds of reasons. They're desperate. They're stalling for time. They need the dough for other things. Or they just don't have it." I shrugged. "If they don't have it, what can you do? You can't get blood from a stone."

"No." Nico grinned. "But you can get blood from a person pretty damn easily."

We continued to crunch through the snow. Most of the warehouse windows had been shattered by vandals. Loops and swirls of graffiti covered the walls. I could hear traffic from the nearby expressway. It was getting dark. Nico walked over to a side door and nudged it open. He looked back at me. "You coming?"

I followed him through the doorway. Inside the warehouse, a lamp, a table, and a chair had been set up. The lamp cast a circle of light on the table and chair. There was a man tied to the chair. His mouth was covered with duct tape and his eyes were bugging out. One side of his face was red and puffy. Two goons I didn't recognize were standing next to the tied-up man. I assumed they worked for DiAngelo.

Nico stepped forward and lifted the man's chin so that they were eye to eye. The man struggled against his ropes and tried to speak. Nico raised his hand to his ear. "What was that? I didn't quite catch that." One of the other goons guffawed.

I took three steps toward the tied-up man. "Just give us the money. This doesn't have to be a problem. You give us the money and we're gone."

The tied-up man looked over at me. His eyes narrowed. He didn't look scared anymore.

Instantly I twisted toward the left, toward Nico. I caught his arm just as he was raising the gun at me. I snapped his arm and the gun went skittering off across the concrete floor. I twisted again, ending up behind Nico just as the other two thugs started shooting. Bullets slammed into

Nico's body. I prayed that the bullets they were using weren't a high enough calibre to punch through Nico into me.

I rushed forward, using Nico's body as a shield. Something nicked my shoulder. At first it felt like a mosquito bite and then it burned like hell. Still holding Nico with one hand, I threw a knife directly into the throat of one of the goons. He gurgled and dropped his gun. The other thug kept shooting until his gun clicked on empty. I pulled out another knife, dropped Nico's body, and rushed the thug.

It was all over within seconds. I stood there, breathing heavily. I didn't know if there were any more goons somewhere watching. Maybe up on the catwalk with a high-powered rifle. But if that were the case, they would've blown my head off the minute I walked through the door. Still, I took cover behind a metal desk.

Nothing. All I could hear were the muffled grunts of the man in the chair. Cautiously, I stepped away from the desk and walked toward him. I ripped the duct tape off his mouth. Nico's body was bleeding at my feet. The two other thugs were crumpled in a heap, limbs sprawled out, half on top of each other.

"Start talking."

"I don't know, man! I didn't see anything, okay? Don't kill me!"

"Who are you?"

"I'm just a guy who owes some money. That's it! I didn't know these guys were going to start shooting!"

The man was lying. I'd seen that look in his eyes when Nico went for his gun. In fact, that look had saved my life. This guy had been in on it from the start.

I hit him, hard. And then I hit him again. Then I hit him again. He slumped forward, unconscious, blood trickling from his mouth. As long as his head stayed where it was, he probably wouldn't drown in his own blood.

I gave my hand a shake and walked out of the warehouse into the snow. As I walked through the parking lot, I reached up and touched my shoulder. A bolt of pain jolted through my body. My fingers came away bloody. I flipped out my phone and punched in Eddie's number. "Meet me outside the supermarket near Cherry Beach. And call Doc Warner, will you? Have her standing by."

"Are you okay?" I could hear the concern in Eddie's voice.

"I think so. Just need a little patching up, is all."

"I'm on it."

Suddenly I was very tired. *Keep walking, Jack.* I wasn't going to die face down in the snow. *Just keep on walking.*

Sooner or later, the tied-up man would wake up. Either he would work his way free, or DiAngelo's boys would drive out to the warehouse, wondering what had happened. I didn't have a whole lot of time left. *Suzanne,* I thought. I called her up. *Keep walking.*

"Hey, babe."

Suzanne's voice crackled on the other end. "Are you okay?"

I'd only said two words and already she had my number.

"I'm fine. I'll be okay. You need to get to Eddie's now. Find Vin. Stay in the casino until I get there."

"I hate it when you order me around."

"I know, and I'm sorry. Please, just do it. We don't have a whole lot of time."

Silence on the other end. Then she said, "All right."

I hoped and I prayed that she'd make it to the casino in time. For all I knew, DiAngelo's goons could be watching her right now.

Eddie came and picked me up. He did some first aid on my shoulder. It hurt like hell. "Looks like the bullet just grazed you. That could've hit your neck or your head."

I grunted as he taped on gauze. "But it didn't. Suzanne's on her way to the casino. We have to go to the mattresses. DiAngelo's going to go to fucking war."

CHAPTER 38

Everyone in the casino was on high alert. Eddie wasn't happy about it, but he had shut the place down. The gamblers would have to find their action elsewhere. The back door to the casino was double-locked. Vin stood next to it, one of Carl's shotguns in his hands. Roger patrolled the front, cradling an Uzi. I wasn't too crazy about guns, and I really wasn't crazy about submachine guns. Those bullets had a tendency to spray like wild. Too easy to hit one of your own, or worse, a random bystander.

Eddie's restaurant upstairs was boarded up with a sign saying Closed for Repairs. Too easy otherwise for DiAngelo's goons to march right in pretending they were just after a steaming plate of chicken balls with red sauce. Eddie had that shit on the menu for the late-night drunks. Now the drunks would have to stagger on farther into the reaches of Chinatown.

Eddie and I and Suzanne sat in Eddie's office. The

big man was sucking on a raspberry lollipop. Suzanne smiled at him. "Sorry about all this, Eddie."

The big man shrugged. "Occupational hazard."

I nodded. "That's a good way to look at it."

He turned to me, a pained expression on his face. "Another way to look at it is that you're costing me money. I need cash flow, Jack. My guys won't work for free."

That wasn't exactly true. I knew Vin and Roger and the rest would lay down their lives for Eddie if need be. They were loyal, almost to a fault.

"Grover's going to deal with DiAngelo."

Suzanne shifted uncomfortably. "I think I'm going to go get a drink. Anyone want anything?"

Eddie nodded. "Scotch. Jack?"

"I'll have a Coke. Thanks, Suzanne."

She left the office. Eddie looked at me and narrowed his eyes. "So what's the freakin' holdup? Grover ices this asshole and we're back in business."

"That's cold, Eddie. That's another human being you're talking about."

He frowned. "War is war, Jack. One side wins and the other side dies."

"Maybe Mario —"

"Mario already went to bat for you once. How'd that work out? It didn't stop the boys in the warehouse, did it?"

He had a point. Mario's days as a peacemaker were over, at least where DiAngelo was concerned.

"Grover was right. DiAngelo was just trying to lure me in so he could shoot me right in the fucking head."

"Don't beat yourself up about it. You knew the score."

I had. I'd known Grover was right all along but had wanted to believe otherwise. I'd wanted that price on my head to vanish into thin air. I'd wanted to take Suzanne by the hand and skip off into the sunset. That was still what I wanted, and I was willing to fight for it.

Eddie crunched up his lollipop and threw away the stick. "I don't like it. We're sitting ducks in here. It's only a matter of time before somebody throws a few sticks of dynamite through the window and *blam.*"

"You boarded up the windows, remember?"

"You know what I mean. If Grover's going to take the fight to DiAngelo, he should do it now."

"I know what he's waiting for."

"What?"

"Grover's planning to hit DiAngelo's counting house and steal his cash before killing him. If he kills DiAngelo first, the counting house gets locked down tight."

Eddie blinked. Slowly, he peeled the cellophane off another lollipop. "Well, shit. How long's that going to take?"

"We're close. We're very close."

"Close don't pay my bills."

"We'll get there, Eddie. Hang on a little longer."

I walked out of the office. Suzanne was sitting on a bar stool. Roger was chatting with her, the Uzi at his side. There was nobody behind the bar. Eddie had told Vivian to go home and stay there until this was all over. Hopefully, that would be soon.

Suzanne saw me coming and stood up. "I'll bring Eddie his Scotch."

"I can do that."

"No problem. I got it." She pointed to the bar. "There's your Coke."

I sipped it. It was sugary and good.

Roger watched Suzanne walk away. I watched him watching her. He turned to me and nodded. "Don't worry, Jack. Any motherfucker tries to break in here, I'll light 'em up like the Fourth of July."

"Are you American?"

"North American. Does that count?"

I turned back to the bar and drank my Coke. I flipped out my phone and punched in the last number I had for Grover. He didn't answer. I knew he swapped out his burners on the regular. I should have been doing the same. I used to just chuck 'em into the lake, but the environmental guilt started to get the best of me. Now I smashed the SIM cards with a hammer and recycled the rest.

The phone rang in my hand. I answered it. "Jack. You recognize my voice?" I did. It was DiAngelo.

"Yeah."

"I heard there were some problems at the warehouse. I want to meet with you, straighten it all out."

I hung up. I trusted DiAngelo about as far as I could throw him. The phone rang again. I sat there drinking my Coke and I let it ring.

Eddie walked across the empty casino floor and sat down next to me. "Phone's ringing, dude."

"Fuck the phone."

Eddie held up his hands. "Okay, okay."

We had only been locked in here about an hour, and I was already going stir crazy. I couldn't just sit here and wait for DiAngelo's goons to come gunning for me.

I stood up. "I'm going out."

Eddie frowned. "What are you, crazy? You know DiAngelo will have guys watching this place."

I cracked my knuckles. "I have to do something."

"It's been an hour, Jack. Cool your jets."

"I know. It's just …" I headed for the door. "I'm going up to my office. Check out the street. That okay with you?"

"Be careful around those windows." The windows in my office were made of bulletproof glass, but even that couldn't stop all bullets. And say DiAngelo got his hands on some military surplus, like some rocket launchers or some shit. Then it would be all over.

Upstairs in my office I gave the plant some water and then I scanned the street. Nothing looked out of the ordinary. Traffic ebbed and flowed. The sky was a smear of grey. A city snowplow trundled up the street.

I felt like I was going to jump out of my skin. I opened up my desk drawer and swapped out some knives. My phone rang again. I flipped it open, ready to curse out DiAngelo. Instead, Eddie was at the other end.

"Doc Warner is here." I had blocked out the pain from my shoulder, but hearing the Doc's name brought it flooding back.

"I'll come right down."

Doc Warner was a good doctor and a good woman. She had patched me up on several occasions. Usually I had to go to her office in Yorkville, but this time she had made an exception.

She stood near the bar in the empty casino. I smiled at her and shook her hand. A bolt of pain shot through my arm.

"All right, Mr. Palace. Let's see that shoulder."

I took off my suit jacket and unbuttoned my shirt. The dried blood on my shoulder stuck the gauze to my skin. I gritted my teeth and yanked it off.

The Doc leaned in. "Mm-hmm. Yes, I see."

"How's it look, Doc?"

"It looks like you got lucky, Mr. Palace. You want a prescription for painkillers?"

I thought of Grover's addicted sister. "No, thanks."

"You sure? They can really take the edge off an injury like this."

"I'm sure."

"All right, then. I'll bandage you up. There might be some nerve damage. The nerves might grow back, or they might not. We'll know more in a few weeks. In the meantime, try to go easy on your right arm." The Doc looked around the empty casino. "Slow day?"

"Something like that."

"We're closed for renovations," Roger put in. The Doc raised her eyebrows but didn't say anything.

I took a wad of bills out of my pocket and peeled off three hundred-dollar bills for the Doc's fee. She pocketed the cash and looked into my eyes. "I don't do this for the money, you know. I want everyone to have the best health care possible. Including you and other people who might not want to go to the hospital."

"I appreciate you coming all the way down here, Doc."

Roger walked Doc Warner out. I went upstairs and got a fresh shirt and a new suit jacket. Maybe bloodstains could be washed out, and maybe a bullet hole could be fixed, but I didn't have time for any of that.

I had said no to the pills, but I wished I hadn't. My shoulder was throbbing with every beat of my heart. I went into the bathroom and opened up my medicine cabinet. Advil would have to do.

There was a knock at the door. I walked over and opened it with my left hand. Suzanne was standing in the doorway, looking sad.

"What's up?"

"Can I come in?"

I stepped aside, and she walked into the room. She leaned against a tower of boxes and looked at me. "Tell me again about the cabin in the woods."

"We'll get there, babe. Sooner than you think."

"Tell me about it, Jack. Will there be kids?"

That was a damn good question. We were both on the older side for having kids, but it was still possible. Sometimes when I pictured the cabin, it was just her and me and nobody else. Sometimes there was a cat, and sometimes there was a dog. And yes, a few times I pictured kids. Not just one, but two or even three, cavorting around on the lawn. "Sometimes I think there might be kids. I mean, I don't know what I'd be like as a father. To tell the truth, the whole idea scares the shit out of me. How about you? When you picture it, are there kids?"

"Yeah." She looked up at me. "Jack, I'm pregnant."

CHAPTER 39

I stood in my office, blinking, my mouth hanging open. Suzanne kept looking at me. "Well? Aren't you going to say something?"

I walked over to her and put my hand on her belly. Then I kissed her, a deep soulful kiss. "We'll make this work, babe. We can make it work."

She still looked sad. "You say that with a bullet wound in your shoulder."

"I won't lie. There's, you know, some obstacles to be overcome. But that's life, right?"

She stared at me with her big dark eyes. "So you'd be happy?"

I gave her belly a pat. "Yes. I mean, I think I am. You're sure about this? It's been less than a week."

Suzanne just smiled.

"And I'm the dad?"

She gave my arm a swat. I grimaced as a jolt of pain shot through me. She winced. "Oh shit, sorry!"

"I'm just asking."

"Yes, you'd be the father, you dipshit." She sighed. "It's too early to tell. It could be nothing. I just ... I wanted to know how you'd feel about it."

I led her over to the couch, and we both sat down. Me, a father. Jack Palace, a dad. "You know I never had a father of my own."

"So you don't have to unlearn any bad habits."

I nodded. "That's a good way to look at it."

"This is going to be a whole new chapter of our lives, Jack. You and me, and baby makes three."

"Unless it's triplets."

"If it's triplets, I'm going to kill you."

"Now, now. Don't make promises you can't keep."

"I swear to God, Jack. If you knocked me up with triplets, I will murder you."

"It wouldn't be so bad. We could name them Huey, Dewey, and Louie. Or Larry, Curly, and Moe."

"We are not naming our babies after the Three Stooges."

"Your loss."

Suzanne playfully swatted me in the head with a pillow.

"Seriously. Twins, triplets, octuplets — we'll make it work."

She leaned in, and we embraced. We stayed that way for a long, long time. Then she broke away. "Do what you've got to do. Just ... come back to me."

I stared into her eyes. "You know I will."

Me, a father. This was a strange, strange world. Still, I supposed stranger things had happened. There was a lot to do before a baby arrived. I had a feeling that nine months would fly by like pages ripped from a calendar in the movies. *Breathe, Jack, breathe. One step at a time.*

Suzanne went back down to the casino. I flipped out my phone to call Grover. "How's it going?"

I could practically hear him grinning on the other end. "Saddle up, Jack. It's time."

CHAPTER 40

Late the next morning, Grover and I drove west to the counting house in a white panel van. Grover was behind the wheel, Max Morris and Dave McDonald were crouched in the back. We were all wearing dark-blue coveralls with white filter masks dangling around our necks. We'd be wearing the masks soon enough.

Grover looked over at me. "There's usually two guys inside the counting house feeding money into the machines. They've got several cash-counting machines in there. When one starts to overheat, they shut it down and use one of the others. Then they stack the cash in the safe. There's a few early morning deliveries but not many. The boys inside go downstairs to the drop-off room, bring the gym bags full of cash back upstairs, count the cash, stack it in the safe, and then they've got nothing to do until the big deliveries start after lunch. I imagine that one guy is supposed to stay in the counting room at all times, but in real life it doesn't work like that. These guys go out for lunch, Jack. Just about every damn day."

"Just about?"

"Nine times out of ten."

"And if today is the tenth?"

Grover smiled. He looked like a shark. "We'll deal with it. These guys go out for lunch, and meanwhile, the deliveries keep happening. They let the bags build up, then they saunter back in and resume the count. We won't bother with the bags on the second floor. The big money is in the safe. Max, that's where you come in."

Max patted the bag of supplies at his feet. "I'm ready."

"There's going to be all kinds of locks on the counting house door. We won't bother with that. We're going in from a neighbouring unit. Single guy, lives alone. This time of day, he'll be at work. The lock on his door is a standard apartment door lock. Max will pop the lock, and then we're in."

I frowned. "The front door of the building is locked, too. Even if we're dressed like workmen, someone on the sidewalk might get suspicious if we're down there picking the lock."

Grover glanced at Max in the rear-view mirror. "Max, show him."

Max dipped into his bag and came up with a key. "You know what this is? It's called a Crown Key. Postal workers carry them. They unlock the front doors of apartment buildings so they can deliver mail to the mail boxes inside. We don't have to pick the front door lock, we can just walk right on inside."

We pulled into a parking spot across the street. We didn't have to wait long. Two men walked out the front door and headed down the street. Grover looked at me and grinned. "There they go. Let's do it."

The key worked just like Max said it would. We trucked into the apartment building carrying our bags of gear, ignored the elevator, and headed for the stairs. Three flights up carrying all our heavy shit, but we weren't about to be boxed in.

Grover peeked around the stairway door. "All clear. Let's move."

My heart was pounding as we walked down the hall. Nothing to see here, ma'am. Just a bunch of maintenance workers doing some repairs on an aging building. Max knelt down at the neighbour's door and picked the lock in about thirty seconds. We all trooped inside. Dave went right up to the wall and started knocking on it softly. He grinned. "These apartment walls are mostly air. You can hear your neighbour's TV. Bad news for them, good news for us." He opened up his black duffle bag and pulled out a Sawzall. The handheld reciprocating saw cut through the drywall like a hot knife through butter.

"Masks on, gents," Grover said. "There's security cameras inside." He dipped into his duffle and came up with two cans of black spray paint. He tossed me one.

Dave cut a square in the wall, about four feet by four. We could've done this job with a drywall knife, but the saw was faster. He packed the Sawzall back into his duffle, and we went through into the counting house.

Mask on, I went over to the security camera over the front door and gave it a squirt. Grover took care of the camera pointing at the safe. There were four counting machines, idle for now, on a long wooden table.

Max went right to the safe. He pulled a burning bar out of his bag and fired it up. The bar glowed orange. He pushed it slowly into the side of the safe.

Grover checked his watch. "C'mon, let's go." He made his voice gruff in case the security cameras were wired for sound.

Liquid metal glowed orange and dripped down the side of the safe. Max grunted. "That should do it." Gloves on, he reached over and pulled the damaged door open.

The money. Stacks and stacks of it. Twenties, fifties, hundreds. Working quickly, we started piling the money into our duffles.

Grover, his bag full, was already over by the hole in the wall. "C'mon, c'mon, c'mon!"

We scrambled through the wall back into the neighbour's apartment. Black futon couch, a television on a stand, a poster of Batman on the wall. Batman wouldn't approve of this, I thought. Together, we all trooped out into the hall. Max locked the neighbour's door behind us. Not quite covering our tracks — there was still a four-by-four-foot hole in the wall between the two apartments. It would be discovered soon enough, but by then we would be long gone.

We walked quickly down the stairs, hoisting our duffle bags full of money and supplies, and right out the back door into the shocking cold of the day. The sun was diffuse yellow, trying to break through the grey murk of the sky. We crunched through the snow toward the van. I thought of those movies where someone gets a pine branch and erases their footprints in the snow. This was a parking lot, though. There were footprints everywhere.

We piled into the van. Adrenaline was running high. We were positively giddy. "Drive!" Max shouted, a smile on his face. "Drive, drive, drive!"

Grover took his time. He didn't peel out of the parking lot, tires squealing. He started the engine and then slowly pulled away.

We took Dundas Street back toward the east end, laughing all the way.

CHAPTER 41

We divvied up the loot at Max's house. There was just over a million dollars. Two hundred and fifty thousand for each of us, with the extra going to Grover. A nice little nest egg. The coveralls got stuffed into Dave's duffle bag. He gave us all a salute as he left. "Gentlemen, it's been a pleasure."

Grover looked at his watch again. "Right about now, those guys are coming back from lunch stuffed with perogies and beer, and they're going to see that hole in the wall."

I frowned. "You think they'll give the neighbour a tough time?"

"They might. But they'll figure out quick that he had nothing to do with it. What're the odds that a safecracker would just happen to have an apartment next to a safe? They'll see that it's a pro job and leave him alone."

I hoped he was right. I didn't want an innocent man getting hurt for something I had done.

Grover shook Max's hand. "Have fun in the casinos, Max. But don't spend it all in one place, okay?"

"Don't you worry about me. I've got a system."

A system. Every gambler thinks he or she has one, and almost every gambler is wrong. The few who do crack a code make millions. Maybe Max would be one of the lucky few but probably not.

"Come on," Grover said to me. "I'll drive you back to Eddie's."

"I won't lie, Jack," Grover said in the car, "I'm happy with how that went down, but I thought there'd be more. I thought two, three million. Two-fifty is nothing to sneeze at, but I thought there'd be more."

I nodded. "I've got to give some of my share to Eddie. Every minute he's closed, he's losing money hand over fist."

Grover reached behind him and grabbed his duffle. "Here, take some of mine."

"I can't do that."

"You can and you will. Go on, take some. All I need is enough to get my sister into rehab." He grinned. "Easy come, easy go. I just can't wait to see the look on DiAngelo's big ugly face."

And there it was. Grover hadn't done it for the money. For him, it was personal. For me, too, I supposed. Sure, the money was nice, but being able to slap back at a guy who had ordered me dead — who had tried to kill me — was sweet, indeed.

"You think your sister will go to rehab?"

"What can I say? I have to at least try."

If DiAngelo was pissed before, he'd be super pissed now. Not that he could prove anything, but a guy like DiAngelo wouldn't worry about that. It wasn't like we were operating in a court of law. Things like proof weren't really necessary. All the man had to do was decide that I'd had something to do with it, and he'd come at me loaded for bear. But fuck it. He was coming anyway, so who gave a shit?

Grover dropped me off in front of Eddie's building. I hoisted my duffle bag off the back seat. I had taken fifty grand of Grover's money for an even three hundred thousand. I'd give Eddie half. Then I'd have one hundred and fifty thousand from the heist and another hundred and fifty thousand — minus Kevin Rhodes's commission — from the sale of The Chief's land. Just under three hundred thousand. Suzanne and I could buy that cabin and have some left over to live on. We couldn't live on it for the rest of our lives, but if we lived cheaply, we could make it last for a long time.

Grover leaned toward the passenger window. "You know what's next, right, Jack? We're going to solve this DiAngelo problem once and for all."

He drove away, leaving me standing in front of Eddie's boarded-up restaurant. All's fair in love and war. DiAngelo had tried to have me killed at least once. In my mind, that meant anything I did to him now was self-defence. Maybe a jury wouldn't see it like that, but like I said, we weren't operating in a court of law.

I spun the keys in the side door, the one that led up to my office and down to the basement. Idly I wondered how long it would take Max Morris to pick these locks. My guess was not long.

I carried my three hundred grand down to the basement. I knocked once, twice, three times, and Roger opened up the door. He was still carting around that Uzi. To tell you the truth, it made me nervous. Roger was a bit of a hothead, and a hothead with a machine gun was a dangerous combination.

Suzanne gave me a kiss. She and Eddie were playing heads-up poker to pass the time. Vin crouched by the back door, cradling his shotgun.

"Can I talk to you?" I said to Eddie. The big man nodded, and together we walked to his office. Inside, I opened up the duffle bag and started stacking cash on his desk.

"What's this?"

"It's money, Eddie. Money can be exchanged for goods and services."

"I know it's money, jackass. Why are you putting it on my desk?"

"It's for you. I know I've severely impeded your cash flow. This is just my way of saying I'm sorry." I kept stacking the cash. "There's a hundred and fifty grand here. That'll cover you for a few days. We're moving into endgame here."

"I'd say I can't take your money, but I'd be lying. I can and I will."

"Good man."

Eddie put the cash in his safe. I thought about Max Morris and his burning bar. If someone wanted in, they could get in. We surrounded ourselves with the illusion of security. That was what helped us sleep at night.

DiAngelo would be hard to get to. Hard but not impossible. I walked out of Eddie's office and sat down next to Suzanne. She looked over at me and smiled. "Good day?"

"So far, so good."

Eddie sauntered back out of his office, too. He sat down opposite Suzanne and they resumed their card game. I watched for a while and then I went up to my office.

The adrenaline from the heist was leaving my system. I wanted to crash on my couch for a while. I kicked off my boots and stretched out. The next thing I knew, I was asleep.

When I woke up, my phone was ringing. "Hello?"

"Jack." I sat up straight. It was Mario. "I heard there's been some trouble. I wanted you to hear it from me personally. I had nothing to do with it."

"I believe you."

"We need to meet."

I didn't say anything. Nico was dead, two other goons were dead. Maybe the guy from Bobby the Beast's bar was dead, as well. All those deaths could be pinned on me. And now here came Mario, a guy who was retired but not really retired, trying to lure me out of my safe house.

"Can you come to me?"

There was a pause on the other end. "I'm old, Jack. You know I don't travel too well these days. But as a show of good faith, I'll make an exception. Don't do anything hasty, okay? We need to talk."

I hung up the phone and glanced over at my plant. "What do you think, Plant? I mean, just what the fuck?" Why in the world was Mario coming to see me? Whatever he had to tell me, it must be important. It was something to do with DiAngelo, that much I could guess. Maybe Mario was trying to keep the man alive. Maybe word had come down from higher up: DiAngelo must be protected.

Or maybe Mario was putting on his nice-guy routine in order to pull the wool over my eyes. He comes over, we meet, one of his bodyguards pulls out a gun, and that's it. Lights out for Jack.

I didn't see it playing out that way, though. Maybe I was an idiot, but Mario had always been straight up with me. It would take him a while to drive from Hamilton into Toronto. I went down to the casino and told Eddie and the gang about our imminent visitor. Suzanne stared at me. "This doesn't sound good, Jack."

Roger was aghast. "He's coming here? Are you fucking kidding me? He's going to bring a fucking army!"

I tilted my chin. "You've got a machine gun. Why are you worried?"

Eddie frowned. "Mario coming here is pretty unusual, Jack. You have to admit that."

"It is strange. It's very, very strange. But he said we — he and I — need to talk. And you know Mario, he's old school. He won't say shit over the phone."

Eddie tapped his head. "He's smart like that."

Suzanne kept staring at me. She had her hand on her belly.

I put my arms around her. "It's going to be all right."

She turned away.

Eddie turned to face Vin and Roger. "We'll set up the meet for the alley. We'll need a guy up on the roof. Vin, that'll be you. Roger will stay here and watch the doors. Jack, I'm coming out with you."

"Nothing doing. I'm coming out alone."

"The hell you are. I'm going to be by your side every step of the way. I'll have my gun, too. Mario and his guys try something, we'll all start shooting."

As a plan, it wasn't the best. "So we all shoot each other. That's your plan?"

"You got a better one?"

"I go out there alone. I talk to Mario and see what he wants. Then we go from there."

"We've got to be ready, Jack."

"Put Vin on the roof. You stay inside with Roger and Suzanne."

"I don't like it."

"I know you don't. But that's the way it's got to be." If I was going down, I wasn't about to take Eddie with me. Vin could retaliate from the rooftop. Spray down bullets into Mario's car. Eddie could sort through the bodies afterward.

Vin and Roger traded guns; Vin got the Uzi and Roger got the shotgun. Vin nodded to me and started to head for the roof. I caught his arm. "It's going to take them a while to drive in from Hamilton. You don't need to be up there freezing your ass off this whole time."

Vin nodded. He went behind the bar and poured himself a Scotch. "You want one?"

I did. I wanted all the Scotch. If I was going to die, I wanted to feel that familiar warmth spreading through my belly one last time. "No, thanks."

The waiting was brutal. We played cards. We listened to the radio. Eddie crunched through about a case of lollipops. Suzanne went into Eddie's office to lie down. Really, it was only about an hour before my phone rang again. "We're about twenty minutes away."

"Good. Pull up behind the building. Call me when you get here."

"Jack, I'm serious. Don't do anything stupid. We're just going to have a conversation, you and me."

"Can't wait."

The last twenty minutes felt like four hours. Roger checked and rechecked the shells in the shotgun. He put another case of ammunition on the bar so he could get to it quickly. Eddie checked his .45. Suzanne came up behind me and kissed my cheek. "You got a lot to live for, Jack."

"I know it." I did know it. I couldn't see a lot of outs without killing DiAngelo, and even that would only dig me in deeper. If Mario had another plan, I was all ears.

My phone rang. "It's me. We're around back."

"Okay. I'm coming out."

Roger opened the back door for me. Snow was swirling down the concrete staircase leading up to the alley. I took a deep breath and headed up.

Mario himself was leaning against the car, hunched in the cold. "I figured you'd want to see me here, and not my driver. I didn't want there to be any misunderstanding."

"You said you needed to talk."

"Actually, you need to listen. All this bloodshed, it's bad for business. It ends now."

I didn't say anything. Mario walked over to the trunk of the car and popped it open. "Come on over here, Jack."

"No, I'm good right here."

Mario smiled. "You think I'm going to get the drop on you? I'm eighty-three years old. You could break me in half like a matchstick."

I took a step closer. My heart was galloping. The hairs on the back of my neck were standing straight up. What if there was a gunman waiting for me in the trunk? I walk over, the gunman opens fire, night-night, Jack.

Mario beckoned me closer. "Come on. I'm not going to bite you."

I took another step and then another. Mario turned away from me and swung the trunk open wide. Someone was in there. I jumped forward, a knife suddenly in my hand.

Mario chuckled. "You won't need that."

I blinked. There in the trunk was Sammy DiAngelo.

CHAPTER 42

The man's hands were zip-tied behind his back. There was blood on the front of his suit. A plastic bag over his head. His face was purple, and his eyes were bugged out, but I could tell it was DiAngelo. Mario's entire trunk was lined with plastic.

I stepped forward, keeping one eye on Mario. I couldn't see his driver past the tinted windows, and that was making me nervous. He might jump out of the car at any minute, guns rattling in his hands.

I gave DiAngelo a poke. He didn't move. I checked for a pulse. His skin was cold. No pulse. The man was dead. Grover was going to be pissed.

Mario looked at me. "You see?"

"I don't understand."

He slammed the trunk closed. "I told you. All this bloodshed is bad for business. We couldn't let this thing drag on forever. It started with" — Mario tilted his chin toward the trunk — "and it ends with him, too."

My head hurt. Too many thoughts were trying to push their way forward. "He said the price on my head didn't come from him."

"He was right about that. Some of my associates, they're not exactly the forgiving type. But I sat down with them. We had a talk. And we agreed. We make one of your problems go away, and you make one of our problems go away."

"What do you mean?"

"There's a man who's been a thorn in our side for a long time. He's a friend of yours. His name is Grover."

I stayed quiet. Mario kept talking. "You see? I do something for you, now you must do something for me."

"I can't kill my friend."

"Friends come and go, Jack. You can always make new friends."

The old man was cold-blooded. But then again, you didn't get to be his age in this business without a certain degree of ruthlessness.

"I can't do it."

Mario sighed. For a ruthless old man, he looked so frail, like a sudden gust of wind could sweep him away. "My associates, they're not as understanding as me. They're a new breed, Jack. It used to be a man's family was considered untouchable." He shook his head. "People don't think that way anymore." He looked up at me. The whites of his eyes were yellow. "I've never met your girlfriend. Suzanne, is that right? I'm sure she's lovely."

I stepped closer to the old man. "Leave her out of this."

"A favour for a favour, Jack. That's all we're asking. After the favour's done, then my associates and I wish you well."

I stood in the cold while Mario got back into his car. The car with the dead man in its trunk drove off. Feeling numb, I walked down the concrete steps to the casino.

Eddie came up to me. "Still alive. That's always a good sign."

"It's a start." I went behind the bar and poured myself a Scotch. Eddie blinked. He didn't say a word. I drank the Scotch. It burned down my throat and into my belly. The familiar warmth spread throughout my body. Goddamn, it was good. I poured myself another.

Kill Grover. Was that my only option? Suzanne and I could pack up our shit and go. Not to the cabin in the woods. Farther this time. The Bahamas. The Cayman Islands. We could raise our baby on the beach. Swimming lessons in the salt water of the ocean. Finally, we could be free.

Except we wouldn't be free, not really. We'd spend the rest of our lives looking over our shoulders. Wondering about every footstep. Cringing at every knock at the door. That was no way to live.

Suzanne looked at me. "Jack?"

I picked up the bottle of Scotch. "I'm going up to the office. Play some more cards with Eddie."

"Jack, what are you doing?"

"Just having a few drinks. Don't worry about me."

"I —"

"I said, don't worry about me."

In my office I paced the floor. I drank Scotch straight from the bottle. It felt like the walls were closing in.

And then I had a moment of clarity. Everything went calm. My breathing slowed. My heart stopped galloping in my chest.

I picked up my phone and punched in a number. "Grover. We need to talk."

CHAPTER 43

The moonlight shone down on the water. Waves lapped at the shore. During the summer days, Ashbridge's Bay was packed with people. At three in the morning on a winter's night, not so much. Grover walked toward me, frowning. "Why the hell did you want to meet way out here? The bar not good enough for you anymore?"

My shoulder hurt. I tossed him a bottle of Scotch with my good arm, and he caught it. "C'mon, Grover," I said. "Have a drink with me."

"You're drinking again?"

"I never really stopped. Not really. Not in my heart."

"Jack, are you drunk?"

"I'm not drunk, but I'm not sober, either."

Grover blinked. He set the bottle down in the sand. "What's wrong?"

"DiAngelo's dead."

"What?"

"Mario and his guys. They killed him."

"Ha ha, Jack. Very funny."

"It's no joke. I saw him, Grover. He was in the trunk of a car. His face was purple."

"DiAngelo's dead?"

"Yup."

Grover raised his hand and then lowered it. "Fuck! Fuck, fuck, fuck." He stepped closer to me. His face was twisted up in a snarl. "I was supposed to kill him. Me!"

"You can't always get what you want."

"You did this. You made some kind of deal."

I shook my head. The waves lapped at the shore. "I was as surprised as you are."

Grover stared out at the lake. "I don't get it. It doesn't make any sense. Unless —" He looked over at me. "They want something from you. Right? They got rid of DiAngelo, and now they want something in return."

I nodded. "You've always been a smart guy, Grover."

"Fuck." He ran his hand through his hair. "I just talked to my sister in Vancouver. I'm going to pay for her to go to rehab. It took some doing, but she agreed to go."

"I hope your sister gets better. I really do."

"Shit, Jack. Fuck." There was a gun in Grover's hand. "They told you to kill me, didn't they?"

My foot lashed out. Grover's gun went flying. The little man ducked under my fist. He jabbed me in the stomach. The air went out of me, and I staggered backwards. "What did they say? They're going to kill you? Kill Eddie? No, I've got it. They're going to kill Suzanne."

I shook my head. "No. I mean, yes, that's what they said. But it doesn't have to be that way. No one needs to die."

"You bastard." Grover charged. I twisted. My fist glanced off his side. His fist slammed into my swollen shoulder. I clamped my teeth down hard and tried not to scream. "What's your plan, then, Jack? You've got a plan, right? Fake my death, maybe? Send them a stranger's finger in the mail? No, that's not your style." He charged again. I deflected. He kicked the knife out of my hand. The deadliest man I had ever met punched me in the stomach again.

I gasped for breath. "This is ... what they want. They want ... us to kill each other."

Grover smiled in the moonlight. "I hate to disappoint them. Only one of us is walking away from this." He charged again. I used his own momentum to flip him up into the air. Somehow, he landed on his feet. I hit him in the face, hard. He rocked backward, feet scrambling in the snowy sand.

I staggered backward, chest heaving. "You can leave. Get on a plane. You retired once. Do it again."

Grover circled, his fists at the ready. "And then what, Jack?"

"Mario's an old man. He's not going to live forever. Someday you can come back."

"And you? And Suzanne?" He stopped and touched his lip. Blood came away on his fingertip. "I don't buy it. You want me dead."

"No. I came to tell you to leave."

Grover shook his head. "They won't stop, Jack. You know that. If they want me dead, they're going to kill me. It's only a matter of time. If you don't kill me, they're going to kill you and everyone else. Eddie. Suzanne. The guy who cuts your hair. Everyone." He had a knife in his hands. The blade gleamed in the moonlight. He rushed me, slicing my sleeve. He kicked me in the stomach, and I went down, falling into the sand and snow.

"Goddammit, Grover, stop! I'm not trying to kill you."

Grover stopped. He was breathing heavily. "It doesn't matter, Jack. I'm already dead. The doctors gave me about three months."

I stepped closer. "What?"

"Lung cancer, you dumb bastard. I'm dying." He lashed out and kicked me in the face.

My ears rang. My vision swam. It was like the vertical hold on a television had gone on the fritz. Grover was three Grovers now.

"Stop ..." A surge of adrenaline hit my body as I scrambled to my feet. Grover was my friend, but he was on the attack. It was kill or be killed. I rushed forward.

The little man tripped me, and I went sprawling in the sand. *This is it*, I thought. *I'm going to die.* Grover stood over me, a knife in his fist. "I always knew it would come down to this. No one will ever know, Jack."

"Wait ..."

"No one will ever know it wasn't you." The blade flashed in the moonlight. The little man reached up and sliced his own throat.

I sat on the beach next to the corpse and watched the waves roll in. Suzanne was safe, that was the important thing. On the other side of the lake, the sun was coming up. Light shimmered on the surface of the water. I looked over at the corpse. "Goodbye," I said. I got to my feet and brushed sand from my pants. Hopefully whoever found the body wouldn't be too traumatized. Early morning joggers or maybe a dog walker, the dog's wet nose sniffing at the body on the beach. I turned my back on the corpse and began trudging through the snow-covered sand.

CHAPTER 44

It was Grover's last gift to me. With his life, he had given me mine. Mario congratulated me on a job well done. I probably looked as sick as I felt.

I got the cheque from the land sale, and Suzanne and I went house hunting. We found a little cabin up near Tobermory. Her belly got bigger by the day. I chopped wood for our wood-burning stove. The months went by, and slowly winter changed to spring.

I thought about failure. I had slipped up back there before I met Grover on the beach, but now I was sober again. Did I miss drinking? I did but less so every day. Palace Security had ultimately failed, as well, but we'd had a few good months. As long as you were living, failure didn't have to be a permanent thing.

I laid my head on Suzanne's belly, and I could hear the baby hiccup. The ultrasound had shown that the baby was a girl. I, Jack Palace, was going to be the father of a beautiful baby girl. We would build a life together.

Maybe not always in the cabin. True freedom wasn't about getting what you wanted, or even being happy with what you had. True freedom was about knowing what you wanted and being able to make a plan to get there. I wanted a nice quiet life with the woman I loved. With my family. Grover, my friend, had made this possible.

Suzanne smiled up at me. "What are you thinking about?"

"Old friends."

"You want to invite Eddie up to the cabin? You guys could get together, talk about old times."

"Sure, let's invite him up." I gave her belly another pat and rolled off the couch. "I don't want to talk about old times, though. I want to talk about new times. What do you say to Eddie being the baby's godfather?"

Suzanne kept smiling. The fire in the stove crackled. "I'd say that makes a lot of sense."

Our firewood supply was getting low. I threw on my coat and headed outside. "Be right back, babe."

The snow was starting to melt. I chopped more wood. The axe bit down, and another log split down the middle.

"Jack?" I looked up. Suzanne was coming toward me, her hand on her belly.

"Everything okay?"

Suzanne took her hand away. "I'm not sure. Are you expecting anyone?" I shook my head. "There's two cars coming up the driveway."

And that's when I realized I would never be free. There would always be more enemies. More threats, more danger, more death. *Suzanne, I'm sorry. I'm so sorry.*

The cars were coming closer. They were long, sleek, and black. Sunlight glinted off the chrome. I picked up my axe, and I went down the drive to meet them.

ACKNOWLEDGEMENTS

Thanks to my agent Kelvin Kong at K2 Literary and thanks to Sam Hiyate at the Rights Factory. Thanks to Scott Fraser, Kendra Martin, Jenny McWha, and the whole gang at Dundurn. Thanks to my editor, Catharine Chen.

Thank you to Geoff Manaugh, whose excellent book *A Burglar's Guide to The City* was a big help while I was researching *Season of Smoke*.

Shout-outs to Iain Deans, Jenny G., Chris Turner, Ashley Bristowe, Beau Levitt, Julia Chan, Jay Lapeyre, Saira Hassan, Matt Stokes, Aaron Chung, Anne Lacoursiere, Anne Yourt, Robin Dwarka, John "J.B." Bauer, Karen Foster, Julie Raymond, Angela Pacini, Sabrina Pacini, Terri Favro, Lisa de Nikolits, Phil Hofton, Conrad Schickedanz, and Jennifer Holloway Flood.

Thanks to my parents, Frances MacFarlane and Don MacFarlane and Don Pasquella. Thanks to Dennis

Boatwright. Thanks to my brother Drew Pasquella. Thanks to my in-laws, Margie and Randy Niedzwiecki. Thanks to my sister-in-law Thaba Niedzwiecki and thanks to my brothers-in-law, Jacob Niedzwiecki, Anand Mahadevan and Phet Sayo.

Thank you with all my heart to my children, Leah and Matthew, and my wife, Emma Niedzwiecki. You three have made my life complete.

ABOUT THE AUTHOR

A.G. Pasquella has been writing stories since he was in grade two. Back then, all his stories were about him somehow getting lots of candy. His range has broadened a bit since then. Still carrying the D.I.Y. ethos of the 80s punk scene, A.G. creates work in many forms: zines, comics, short stories, novellas, novels, and music. His band Miracle Beard, created with co-founder Ron Cunnane, has released ten albums and counting. His work has appeared in *McSweeney's*, *Black Book*, *Imaginarium 2013: The Best Canadian Speculative Writing*, *Joyland*, and *Little Brother*, among other publications. He is the co-editor (with Terri Favro) of *PAC'N HEAT: A Noir Homage to Ms. Pac-Man*. Born in Dallas, Texas, A.G. has lived in Toronto for the past twenty years.

CPSIA information can be obtained
at www.ICGtesting.com
Printed in the USA
JSHW031523030221
11535JS00002B/51